Carlyle's House

Carlyle's House

and Other Sketches

Virginia Woolf

Edited by David Bradshaw

ET REMOTISSIMA PROPE

100 PAGES

100 PAGES
Published by Hesperus Press Limited
4 Rickett Street, London sw6 1RU
www.hesperuspress.com

ISBN: 1-84391-055-1

CONTENTS

FOREWORD

These pieces are like five-finger exercises for future excellence. Not that they are negligible, being lively, and with the direct and sometimes brutal observation, the discrimination, the fastidious judgement one expects from her... but wait: that word 'judgement' – it will not do. Virginia Woolf cared very much about refinement of taste, her own and her subjects'. 'I imagine that her taste and insight are not fine; when she described people she ran into stock phrases, and took rather a cheap view.' ('Miss Reeves') This note is struck often throughout her work, and because of her insistence one has to remember that this woman, in February 1910, took part in a silly jape, pretending to be of the Emperor of Abyssinia's party on a visit to a British battleship; that she and her friends went in for the naughty words you would expect from school-children who have just discovered smut; that she was to some extent anti-Semitic, capable of referring to her admirable and loving husband as 'the Jew'. The sketch here, 'Jews', is an unpleasant piece of writing. But then you have to remember a similarly noisy and colourful Jewess in *Between the Acts* described affectionately – Woolf likes her. So this writing here is often unregenerate Woolf, early work pieces, and some might argue they would have been better left undiscovered. Not I: it is always instructive to see what early crudities a writer has refined into balance – into maturity.

None of that lot, the Bloomsbury artists, can be understood without remembering that they were the very heart and essence of Bohemia, whose attitudes have been so generally absorbed it is hard to see how sharply Bohemia stood out against its time. They are sensitive and art-loving, unlike their enemies and opposites, the crude business class. E.M. Forster,

Virginia Woolf's good friend, wrote *Howards End*, where the battle between Art and the Wilcoxes is set out. On the one hand the upholders of civilisation, on the other, philistines, the 'Wilcoxes'. To be sensitive and fine was to fight for the survival of real and good values, against mockery, misunderstanding and, often, real persecution. Many a genuine or aspiring Bohemian was cut off by outraged parents.

But it was not only 'the Wilcoxes', crass middle-class vulgarians, but the working people who were enemies. The snobbery of Woolf and her friends now seems not merely laughable, but damaging, a narrowing ignorance. In Forster's *Howards End* two upper-class young women, seeing a working person suffer, remark that 'they' don't feel it in the same way – as I used to hear white people, when they did notice the misery of the Blacks, say, 'They aren't like us; they have thick skins.'

With Woolf we are up against a knot, a tangle of unlikeable prejudices, some of her time, some personal, and this must lead us to look again at her literary criticism, which was often as fine as anything written before or since, and yet she was capable of thumping prejudice, like the fanatic who can see only his own truth. Delicacy and sensitivity in writing was everything and that meant Arnold Bennett, and writers like him, were not merely old hat, the despised older generation, but deserved obloquy and oblivion. Virginia Woolf was not one for half measures. The idea that one may like Arnold Bennett *and* Virginia Woolf, Woolf *and* James Joyce was not possible for her. These polarisations, unfortunately endemic in the literary world, always do damage: Woolf did damage. For decades the arbitrary ukase dominated the higher reaches of literary criticism. (Perhaps we should ask why literature is so easily influenced by immoderate opinion?) A fine writer,

Arnold Bennett, has to be rejected, apologised for, and then – later – passionately defended, in exactly her own way of doing things: attack or passionate defence. Bennett: good; Woolf: bad. But I think the acid has leaked out and away from the confrontation.

A recent film, *The Hours*, presents Woolf in a way surely her contemporaries would have marvelled at. She is the very image of a sensitive suffering lady novelist. Where is the malicious spiteful woman she in fact was? And dirty-mouthed, too, though with an upper-class accent. Posterity, it seems, has to soften and make respectable, smooth and polish, unable to see that the rough, the raw, the discordant, may be the source and nurse of creativity. It was inevitable that Woolf would end up as a genteel lady of letters, though I don't think any of us could have believed she would be played by a young, beautiful, fashionable girl who never smiles, whose permanent frown shows how many deep and difficult thoughts she is having. Good God! the woman enjoyed life when she wasn't ill; liked parties, her friends, picnics, excursions, jaunts. How we do love female victims; oh, how we do love them.

What Virginia Woolf did for literature was to experiment all her life, trying to make her novels nets to catch what she saw as a subtler truth about life. Her 'styles' were attempts to use her sensibility to make of the living the 'luminous envelope' she insists our consciousness is, not the linear plod she perceived writing like Bennett's to be.

Some people like one book, others another. There are those who admire *The Waves*, her most extreme experiment, which to me is a failure, but a brave one. *Night and Day* was her most conventional novel, recognisable by the common reader, but she attempted to widen and deepen it. From her first novel, *The Voyage Out*, to the last, the unfinished *Between the Acts* –

which has for me the stamp of truth; I remember whole passages, and incidents of a few words or lines seem to hold the essence of, let's say, old age, or marriage, or how you experience a much-loved picture – her writing life was a progression of daring experiments. And if we do not always think well of her progeny – some attempts to emulate her have been unfortunate – then without her, without James Joyce (and they have more in common than either would have cared to acknowledge) our literature would have been poorer.

She is a writer some people love to hate. It is painful when someone whose judgement you respect comes out with a hymn of dislike, or even hate, for Virginia Woolf. I always want to argue with them: but how can you not see how wonderful she is... For me, her two great achievements are *Orlando*, which always makes me laugh, it is such a witty little book, perfect, a gem; and *To the Lighthouse*, which I think is one of the finest novels in English. Yet people of the tenderest discrimination cannot find a good word to say. I want to protest that surely it should not be 'the dreadful novels of Virginia Woolf', 'silly *Orlando*', but rather '*I* don't like *Orlando*', '*I* don't like *To the Lighthouse*', '*I* don't like Virginia Woolf'. After all, when people of equal discrimination to oneself, adore, or hate the same book, the smallest act of modesty, the minimum act of respect for the great profession of literary critic should be, '*I* don't like Woolf, but that is just my bias.'

Another problem with her is that when it is not a question of one of her achieved works, she is often on an edge where the sort of questions that lurk in the unfinished shadier areas of life are unresolved. In this collection is a little sketch, called 'A Modern Salon', about Lady Ottoline Morrell, who played such a role in the lives and work of many of the artists and writers of her time, from D.H. Lawrence to Bertrand Russell.

We are glad to read what Woolf thinks, when so many others have had their say. Woolf describes her as a great lady who has become discontented with her own class and found what she wanted in artists, writers. They see her as 'a disembodied spirit escaping from her world into a purer air'. And, 'she comes from a distance, with strange colours upon her.' That aristocrats had, and in some places still have, glamour, we have to acknowledge, and here Woolf is trying to analyse it and its effects on 'humbler creatures', but there is something uncomfortably sticky here; she labours on, sentence after sentence, until it seems she is trying to stick a pin through a butterfly's head. There were few aristocrats in the Bohemian world of that time: it is a pity Ottoline Morrell was such a bizarre representative of it. A pitiful woman, she seems now, so generous with money and hospitality to so many protégés, and betrayed and caricatured by many of them. They don't come out very well, the high-minded citizens of Bohemia, in their collision with money and aristocracy.

It is hard for a writer to be objective about another who has had such an influence – on me, on other women writers. Not her styles, her experiments, her sometimes intemperate pronouncements, but simply, her existence, her bravery, her wit, her ability to look at the situation of women without bitterness. And yet she could hit back. There were not so many female writers then, when she began to write, or even when I did. A hint of the hostilities confronted is in her sketch here of James Strachey and his Cambridge friends. '...I was conscious that not only my remarks but my presence was criticized. They wished for the truth, and doubted whether a woman could speak it or be it.' And then the wasp's swift sting: 'I had to remember that one is not full grown at 21.'

I think a good deal of her waspishness was simply that:

women writers did not, and occasionally even now do not, have an easy time of it.

We all wish our idols and exemplars were perfect; a pity she was such a wasp, such a snob – and all the rest of it, but love has to be warts and all. At her best she was a very great artist, I think, and part of the reason was that she was suffused with the spirit of 'They wished for the truth' – like her friends, and indeed, all of Bohemia.

– Doris Lessing, 2003

INTRODUCTION

The first entry in this early journal opens with Virginia Woolf
– Virginia Stephen as she was at the time – finding herself
where she did not want to be. There was much to preoccupy
Woolf on and around Shrove Tuesday 1909 (23rd February)
and it is tempting to imagine her engrossed in her thoughts
and oblivious to her surroundings as she journeyed from
central London to Carlyle's House, Chelsea, the former home
of the great man of letters. While her being taken 'too far'
might simply be explained by the absence of a bus-stop where
Woolf had expected one, at the time she began this journal she
was unquestionably some distance from where she wished
to be vocationally, domestically and emotionally.

By February 1909 Woolf had already been struggling with
her first novel for well over two years and it would be another
six before it was published. In addition, circumstances had
forced her to share a house (29, Fitzroy Square) with her
brother, Adrian, in what Hermione Lee has called an 'unsatis-
factory *ménage à deux*'.[1] But most distracting of all, perhaps,
as she made her way westwards on 23rd February, was her
awareness of her unchanged marital status. A few days earlier,
on 17th February, Woolf and Lytton Strachey had suddenly
agreed to get married and then almost immediately (and
wisely) had second thoughts.[2] For some time she had been
urged to get married by more or less everyone who knew her
well, yet her acceptance of the first proposal she'd received
had ended in fiasco. As she alighted from her bus beyond

1. Hermione Lee, *Virginia Woolf* (London: Chatto and Windus, 1996), p. 305.
Cited hereafter as Lee.
2. Michael Holroyd, *Lytton Strachey* (London: Chatto and Windus, 1994),
pp. 200–2; Lee, pp. 259–61.

Carlyle's House, Woolf may well have reflected that she had also gone 'too far' less than a week before. And, if this thought did cross her mind, she must have been even more painfully conscious, following her mutual '*éclaircissement*' with Strachey on 20th February,[3] of just how displaced and unfulfilled she remained. Paradoxically, Woolf had gone both a tad 'too far' and absolutely nowhere in the last few days.

Two years earlier, she would have been able to fall back on her 'complex, many-layered'[4] intimacy with Vanessa, her elder sister and soulmate. But Vanessa was now a married woman and mother (her first child, Julian, was born on 4th February 1908), still resident at 46, Gordon Square, the capacious house in Bloomsbury where Virginia, Vanessa, Adrian and their brother Thoby (until his death in November 1906) had lived as an orphaned menagerie (their mother had died in 1895 and their father in 1904) between late 1904 and 1907. It was when Vanessa married Clive Bell on 7th February 1907 that Woolf and Adrian had had to leave Gordon Square and move to Fitzroy Square, but even though two years had elapsed and she saw her sister regularly, Virginia still missed living with Vanessa just as intensely as she disliked living alone with the awkward and unsympathetic Adrian. Her sister, moreover, was beginning to find success in her own vocation, painting, while Woolf, for all her regular work as a reviewer, did not feel she was making much progress at all as a writer. When she submitted her first piece of fiction to a national magazine later in the year (she sent 'Memoirs of a Novelist' to the *Cornhill* in October 1909), it was rejected. What 'could have been momentous in the history of Virginia's development as a

3. Holroyd, *Lytton Strachey*, p. 202.
4. Jane Dunn, *A Very Close Conspiracy: Vanessa Bell and Virginia Woolf* (London: Jonathan Cape, 1990), p. 1.

writer', was in the event just a flop. [5]

That autumnal rejection slip encapsulates all that was off-key for Woolf in 1909, particularly in the first and last quarters of the year, and her underlying sadness and dissatisfaction during the period this journal covers must at least partially account for its distinctly edgy grain. Readers hoping to be engirdled by the sardonic, spicy, humane, mischievous, quirky and sagacious diarist who holds sway in Anne Olivier Bell's five-volume edition of *The Diary of Virginia Woolf* (1977–84) will feel a little rebuffed. That diary begins in 1915 (and ends with Woolf's death in 1941), but the author of this 1909 journal, while (on the whole) characteristically penetrating, candid, ruminative, lyrical, idiosyncratic and engrossing, can also come across as judgemental, cutting (especially in 'A Modern Salon'), over-precise, prickly, rather pompous (especially in 'Cambridge' and 'Hampstead') and, in one of the sketches, 'Jews', plainly offensive.

Though the tartness of 'Jews' is unparalleled in the volume, displaying a nasty (if conventional) streak of anti-Semitism on Woolf's part, her disparagement of Mrs Annie Loeb is best seen, perhaps, as part of the journal's pervasive mood of captiousness. Woolf is snobbishly quick to deem people 'coarse' (as well as Mrs Loeb, Sir George Darwin's wife in 'Cambridge' and Miss Lewis in 'Divorce Courts' are also dismissed in this way) and there is a general tendency to fault-find in the sketches. Woolf's description of Lady Ottoline Morrell's appearance and her analysis of her party-giving in 'A Modern Salon', for instance, contrive to be both spot on and spiteful.

As she matured as a writer, Woolf grew to relish the fugitive imponderability of life – it is a delight which beams out from

5. Quentin Bell, *Virginia Woolf: A Biography (Volume i: Virginia Stephen 1882–1912)* (London: Hogarth Press, 1973), p. 153. Hereafter, Bell, i.

her short story 'An Unwritten Novel' and from *Mrs Dalloway*, for instance – whereas in 'Miss Reeves', 'Cambridge' and 'Divorce Courts' there is something akin to smugness in the way she recalls her experiences and inscribes her opinions. She captures her subject, as it were, without a chance of it getting away, like one of the moths that she and her siblings used to collect as children during their summer vacations in St Ives.

On 25th January 1909 Woolf had turned twenty-seven, the age her beloved half-sister Stella had been on her wedding day in 1897,[6] and her sense of the significance of her age, coupled with the emotional fallout of her momentary 'engagement' to Strachey, may help to explain why the theme of marriage and its alternatives is so prominent in these sketches. In the opening piece, Woolf puzzles intently over the marital dynamics of Mr and Mrs Thomas Carlyle, and in the second she is both entranced by the snaky sexiness of the unmarried Amber Reeves and snooty about her lack of 'mystery'. She assays the spinsterly harmony of the 'Misses Case' with a warmth which never quite quickens into unalloyed admiration in 'Hampstead', and she reflects coolly on the physical and emotional cost of Margaret Llewelyn Davies' long dedication to the Women's Co-operative Guild in the same sketch: 'Women who have worked but have not married,' she writes, 'come to have a particular look; refinement, without sex; tending to be austere.' All the more fitting, then, that the 'not married' Woolf should dissect the marriage of Sir George Darwin and his wife in 'Cambridge' with a somewhat 'austere' eye. She is acerbic, in 'Jews', about what she takes to be Mrs Loeb's 'one end' for the young women of her acquaintance and her poor relations – 'the society of men and marriage' –

6. Stella Duckworth also died in 1897, only three months after her marriage to John Waller ('Jack') Hills.

and in 'Divorce Courts' she listens attentively as the bones of a marriage are laid bare. 'It seemed to show one real married life,' she writes of her day in court, 'the kind of humdrum, genuine relationship it is; the human beings so real, giving each other a little comfort, having worn through all disguises and both heavy laden.'

While it would be a gross distortion to suggest that Woolf was obsessed with her marital status in 1909, the issue of marriage was undoubtedly near the forefront of her mind during the year, and it is a concern which her journal reflects. Two years later (she did not marry Leonard Woolf until 1912), comparing her own position with Vanessa's, Woolf wrote dispiritedly of the 'hairy black' devils of depression which had plagued her during a London summer storm: 'To be 29 and unmarried – to be a failure – childless – insane too, no writer.'[7] Her ordering of her 'devils' is suggestive.

As the title of this volume indicates, Woolf's 1909 journal is by no means a daily record of events and/or reflections. Like her other early journals of the 1897–1909 period, brought together and edited by Mitchell A. Leaska in 1992, Woolf's 1909 notebook (which would have been included in Leaska's volume, presumably, had its existence been known about) functioned primarily as a verbal sketch-book. Indeed, it shares many of the characteristics and served the same broad purpose as her 1903 journal, about which Woolf commented:

'…I wish for the sake of this book that I had anything more brightly coloured & picturesque to write here; it seems to me that all my events have been of the same temperate

7. Nigel Nicolson and Joanne Trautmann, eds, *The Flight of the Mind: The Letters of Virginia Woolf (Volume i: 1888–1912)* (London: The Hogarth Press, 1983), p. 466. Hereafter, *Letters*, i.

rather cold hued description; I haven't had to use many superlatives. I have sketched faint outlines with a pencil. But the only use of this book is that it shall serve for a sketch book; as an artist fills his pages with scraps & fragments, studies of drapery – legs, arms & noses – useful to him no doubt, but of no meaning to anyone else – so I… take up my pen & trace here whatever shapes I happen to have in my head…

It is an exercise – training for eye & hand – roughness if it results from an honest desire to put down the truth with whatever materials one has to hand, is not disagreeable – though often I am afraid decidedly uncouth.'[8]

Six of the seven sketches which comprise *Carlyle's House* might be described as 'rough', but they also exert the same pull and reveal many of the same qualities as Woolf's most accomplished work. The seventh sketch, 'Jews', *is* 'disagreeable', there can be no argument about that. Indeed, Woolf's denigration of Mrs Loeb might be branded 'decidedly uncouth'.

And all the pieces, including 'Jews', could be characterised as 'rather cold hued'. There are few 'superlatives' employed here, perfectly befitting a period in Woolf's life which was not, for all its social distractions, either 'brightly coloured' or 'picturesque' or satisfying. Nor, in many ways, is the 1909 journal anything like as full, varied or revealing as the previously published journals of 1897, 1899, 1903–8, or the one Woolf kept in April and May 1909 during her vacation in Italy. On the other hand, what more graphic record could such an eventually prolific and assured writer have left of a year in

8. Virginia Woolf, *A Passionate Apprentice: The Early Journals 1897–1909* ed. Mitchell A. Leaska (London: The Hogarth Press, 1990), pp. 186–7. Hereafter, *A Passionate Apprentice*.

which she was generally unhappy and in which she failed to make any real progress with her novel, than a journal in which the majority of the pages are blank and the tone is subdued? For one reason or another, 1909 was not a vintage year for 'diarising',[9] as Woolf called it, but this makes what she did write all the more fascinating.

If the young woman we meet here is someone whose refinement fits her too tightly in places and who is too ready to pass judgement on others, we also encounter Woolf in one of her most familiar and engaging aspects: all seven sketches bear witness to her life-long determination to get to the bottom of things, 'to write not only with the eye, but with the mind; & discover real things beneath the show,' as she put it in her Italian journal of 1908.[10] They provide new evidence of Woolf's enduring professional urge to train her 'eye & hand', to pick up her pen and record anything which might one day be of use in her fiction:

'...I shall try to be an honest servant, gathering such matter as may serve a more skilled hand later – or suggest finished pictures to the eye.

The fact is, that in these private books, I use a kind of shorthand, & make little confessions, as though I wished to propitiate my own eye, reading later.'[11]

Does the 'peppery' Sir George Darwin contribute anything to the irascible Cambridge don William Pepper in *The Voyage Out*? And did Woolf recall, as now seems likely, Sir George's solicitous concern with women's shoes as she wrote the scene

9. *A Passionate Apprentice*, p. 121.
10. *A Passionate Apprentice*, p. 384.
11. *A Passionate Apprentice*, pp. 384-5.

in *To the Lighthouse* when the elderly botanist William Bankes sidles over to Lily Briscoe and comments on what she has on her feet? 'Her shoes were excellent, he observed. They allowed the toes their natural expansion.'[12] There is definitely something of Margaret Llewelyn Davies in the characters of Mary Datchet in *Night and Day* and Eleanor Pargiter in *The Years*, and there's much of Janet Case in *The Years*'s Lucy Craddock, but it is interesting to note that nowhere in Woolf's fiction is there a version of the young, seductive and ophidian Amber Reeves.

Although the often witty Woolf of the later diary and letters is not much in evidence in this journal, we do catch glimpses of her. For instance, her silent retort to the estranging self-absorption of James Strachey and Rupert Brooke during her 'very difficult duet' with H.T. J. Norton in 'Cambridge' – 'I had to remember that one is not full grown at 21' – puts them firmly in their place, while earlier in the same sketch Woolf likens Sir George Darwin to 'some elderly but wiry grey terrier, with short legs, and choleric eyes, rather watering at the corners'. But though there are images and passages to smile at in this journal, its readers are unlikely to roar their way through it from beginning to end.

'It's one of the peculiarities of [Woolf's] posthumous reputation,' her most authoritative biographer has remarked, 'that the full, immense extent of her life's work has only revealed itself gradually, changing the... perception of her from the delicate lady authoress of a few experimental novels and sketches, some essays and a "writer's" diary, to one of the most professional, perfectionist, energetic, courageous and committed writers in the language.'[13] This 1909 journal reveals

12. Virginia Woolf, *To the Lighthouse* ed. Stella McNichol (Harmondsworth, Middlesex: Penguin Books, 1992), p. 22.
13. Lee, p. 4.

something of all these qualities as well as some less attractive ones, and it is a substantial addition to the Woolf canon, not least because it provides further evidence of Woolf's state of mind during a year of 'many vexations and disappointments'.[14] It is also valuable because it extends our knowledge of Woolf's movements, contacts and social activities in 1909 and because all seven of the sketches relate either to major figures or key issues in her life and work, or to aspects of her writings which her critics have singled out for attention, either to her credit or detriment. They shed further light, for example, not only on Woolf's anti-Semitic prejudice, but also on her ongoing relationship with the shades of Jane and Thomas Carlyle (in their different ways, key figures in her development as a writer) as well as providing new angles on such prime Woolfian concerns as patriarchy, feminism and marriage.

Furthermore, if Lee is correct in her assertion that a central preoccupation of Woolf's writing was 'the concept of not belonging, of alienation',[15] then this journal reinforces her take on the novelist. The general impression which comes across, arguably, is of a rather discontented and crotchety Woolf who only felt inspired to write in her journal sporadically. But if this impression is accurate, then the author of this journal speaks powerfully for the tiro writer who was immured in a house with a difficult brother on a different wavelength in 1909 and who fretted about marriage and her novel being stalled.

However, if we are inclined to register the journal's impact in this way, we should not allow its tone and content to blind us to the fact that Woolf, like all really great artists, was as

14. Bell, i, p. 154.
15. Lee, p. 226.

elusive and as irreducible as the life she wrote about. For at almost exactly the same time as she entered the vitriolic 'Jews' in her journal, which most readers will recoil from as the outpouring of a sour and embittered woman and some will find simply unpalatable, Ray Costelloe describes a gathering at 29, Fitzroy Square which shows Woolf in a quite different light:

> 'We sat around the fire in anything but gloomy silence... in fact we talked continuously of diseases and shipwrecks and other frivolous topics. Then we somehow fell to making noises at the dog, and this awe-inspiring company might have been seen leaping from chair to chair uttering wild growls and shrieks of laughter... Virginia... was very friendly and told me about the way she lives and the people she meets and the things that seem important.'[16]

Of course, this snapshot of Woolf does not dispel the affront of a piece like 'Jews', but it does remind us of something she would go on to emphasise in her greatest novels (and which her readers must never forget): no one is *simply* anything, be it an anti-Semite or a feminist trail-blazer. Later on in her life, in the 1930s, Woolf would not only write a philo-Semitic novel (*The Years*), but would subject her own bigotry and that of her class to close and painful scrutiny. What we have here are sketches from Woolf's noviciate as a writer; they are by no means the full story.

Tucked into the back of the notebook, when it was rediscovered, was a letter to Woolf from her close friend the composer, feminist and suffragette Ethel Smyth (1858–1944).

16. Quoted in Barbara Strachey, *Remarkable Relations: The Story of the Pearsall Smith Family* (London: Gollancz, 1981), pp. 247–8.

Dated 15th January 1939, it is a possible pointer to when the diary was last handled by Woolf. It could be that she was at one point toying with the idea of extending her 'Sketch of the Past', her most expansive autobiographical work, begun in 1939, as far as the events of 1909 (in particular Strachey's proposal) and beyond. In the event she didn't, but this previously unpublished letter from Smyth is so idiosyncratically diffuse and affectionate that it is worth giving a taste of it. It is also interesting to contrast Smyth's projection of the almost legendary Virginia Woolf of 1939 with the Virginia Stephen we meet in this 1909 journal.

The autograph letter is written in green ink and is praised by Woolf in her letter to Smyth of 24th January 1939: 'I knew I didn't deserve a letter, as I never answered the long one – the charming one – the one that jumped and tumbled and wandered in and out of corners that you wrote the other day. But... well you know my habits as a letter writer, so I'll say no more.'[17] True to Woolf's description of it, Smyth's letter begins *in medias res* and is as acrobatic and as meandering, as dense and as 'charming' as she says:

' "Yes" I said to Miss Margaret Lane who was staring this time yesterday at your photo, "I think sometimes she's the most beautiful person I ever saw – but then that's the type of beauty I admire most." And I began talking of Virginia, for Lane has real deep admiration for your writings and is a very intelligent girl, really a "Mrs Wallace" – hence her writing recently an excellent life of that big bounder her

17. Nigel Nicolson and Joanne Trautmann, eds, *Leave the Letters Till We're Dead: The Letters of Virginia Woolf (Volume vi: 1936–1941)* (London: The Hogarth Press, 1980), p. 311. Hereafter, *Letters*, vi.

father in law.[18] Isn't it lucky that though I didn't know this (she sent me the book "on the chance I might read it by mistake") that I only said "I *will* read it!" Tho' I confess E.[dgar] W.[allace] is not a hero of mine. I think it very clever of her to have written a book that gives you a picture of the awful creature he was, yet makes you rather like him (at off moments) and has not embroiled her with the Wallace Family. "The odd thing about V.W. is" – I said – "that she gives 1/4 of an inch, well aware that she'll get an ell[19]." And I said this skinflint of a woman puts it across every time – partly because you know that if she gave 3/8 of an inch it would knock her up, and partly because what she does give has a quality beyond the price of rubies. I told her that you live as much as you can on silence all day, dinner parties at which you look too lovely for words and are supremely entertaining and funny, and cannot work many hours in the day. She was, as I always am, staggered at what you get through in the year all the same…

…Yes, Virginia, I'm on the loose. I sent off yesterday the second instalment of my book, to be typed.[20] That'll be about 12000 words I think. Betty[21] very satisfactory. I pay attention to her and as she looked sad over my account of being ravished in Paris I asked her whether she disliked it? (I said nothing about the vaseline – only that I thought certain new departures, like skiing for instance, should be embarked on young, while your muscles are yielding, etc.)

18. Margaret Lane, *Edgar Wallace: The Biography of a Phenomenon* (London: William Heinemann, [1938]). Edgar Wallace (1875–1932) was the author of over 170 popular novels and detective stories.
19. About 45 inches.
20. *What Happened Next* (1940).
21. Probably Lady Balfour, a close friend of Smyth in her later years.

Well, Betty said she thought it was rather ugly, and she's not a bit of a prude, tho' in some ways a little "old fashioned grandam" in her feelings. So I left that out. Not the violation but the treatment – the angle, etc and Vita's[22] remark about the sinfulness of not having an anaesthetist present...

...I loved your letter[23] and am glad you let your mother in law want to go on living at 88. Though how she can beats me...'

It seems appropriate to end the Introduction with this reminder of how Woolf was seen by a close and adoring friend when she was at the pinnacle of her fame (and at a time when we know she was deeply conscious of the perils of Nazism). For although this 1909 journal provides us with new glimpses of Woolf and new perspectives on her life, it also discloses a Woolf who offends. But this more censorious, even, at times, unpleasant Woolf should not, cannot be censored. Unmuzzled and untempered, the diarist of 1909 must take her place alongside the more unproblematic, sympathetic and iconic Virginia Woolfs of the past century.

– *David Bradshaw, 2003*

---

22. Vita Sackville-West (1892–1962).
23. *Letters*, vi, p. 309, in which Woolf tells Smyth: 'My mother in law... has once more bobbed to the top. As she longs to live, at 88, why not? The family begins to treat her as a cricketer doing a record score. All grievances silenced. Can she make 100? I daresay.'

NOTE ON THE TEXT

The journal takes the form of a quarto holograph notebook of 214 pages, bound (almost certainly by Woolf herself) in brown paper. She has written '1909' on the front cover in green pencil or crayon. The recto pages are hand-numbered, and the first such page (for reasons which are not entirely clear) is numbered '26'. At the centre of page 26 is written, again in Woolf's hand: 'Feb: 27th 1909'. On p. 27 there is a contents list which gives the relevant page number on which each sketch begins. Pagination continues up to p. 50, with pp. [51] and [52] being the last two pages on which anything is written. The remaining pages are unnumbered and blank. All entries are in blue/black ink on pale cream feint-ruled paper. The notebook measures 207 x 167 mm.

The entries in the notebook contain only a few deletions and none of these are substantial or in any way significant. For this edition, light punctuation has been added here and there to aid sense. The most obvious example of this is my decision to change the title of the first sketch (and, indeed, of the volume as a whole) from Woolf's 'Carlyles House' to 'Carlyle's House'. Woolf's use of apostrophes in contracted forms and in the possessive case was never strictly conscientious.

Occasionally it is difficult to decide whether Woolf has used a comma, a colon or a semicolon, and in cases where the punctuation is unclear or illegible I have chosen the symbol which seems most appropriate to the sense of the passage in question. A small number of paragraph breaks have been introduced, again with the intention of accentuating the sense of the text.

Finally, 'Jews' and 'Divorce Courts' appear under the same title in the notebook ('Jews and Divorce Courts') with a clear break in the text between 'and very unpleasant' (the last words of 'Jews' in this edition) and 'Curiosity took me' (the opening words of 'Divorce Courts'). Since the two sketches are entirely unconnected and Woolf's title is misleading, I have decided to separate them into two distinct sketches for this edition – even though by doing so 'Jews' is brought into even sharper focus.

In the years after Woolf's death in 1941 her husband, Leonard, saw to it that all her holograph notebooks, her diary and her letters were transcribed and typed up before he sold them. So what happened to this notebook and where has it been?

One of the people he asked to type up material was a young woman named Teresa Davies, née David. Her husband, Professor Tony Davies takes up the story:

'In 1968, when we were newly married and living in rural indigence and discomfort in mid-Wales, Teresa was eking out a student income by taking on occasional typing jobs. Some of these were for Leonard Woolf (procured, I'd guess, by his devoted companion Trekkie Parsons, who was an old friend of Teresa's parents, Dick and Nora David[1]). Some time that year he sent her a notebook re-covered in brown paper, dated 1909... Before Teresa had set about typing this up, Leonard became ill and died, and, uncertain what to do with the notebook, she put it away in a bottom drawer, where... it remained forgotten until our recent move...'[2]

The notebook is now housed as part of the Monks House Papers in the Special Collections section of the University of Sussex Library, Brighton.

1. See Judith Adamson, ed., *Love Letters: Leonard Woolf and Trekkie Ritchie Parsons (1941–1968)* (London: Chatto and Windus, 2001), pp. 234 and 280.
2. Tony Davies to David Bradshaw, 10th September 2002.

ACKNOWLEDGEMENTS

I am deeply indebted to the Estate of Virginia Woolf for granting me permission to prepare this edition of Woolf's 1909 journal for the press. In particular, I would like to thank Jeremy Crow and Elizabeth Haylett of the Society of Authors, and Jenny Rayner of Hesperus Press, for expediting the project and being supportive throughout.

As in all fields of research, only star-blessed prodigies get anywhere on their own. The following people have all gone out of their way to provide me with assistance of one kind or another and this volume would be much the poorer without their input. I am extremely grateful to: Stephen Barkway of the Virginia Woolf Society of Great Britain; Olivier Bell, Professor Ian Campbell; the ever-dependable Stuart Clarke of the VWSGB; Tony Davies; Oliver Davies; Professor John Deathridge; Robert Fearnley-Whittingstall; Christopher Fifield; the ever-indispensable Bet Inglis; David Loeb; Sylvia Loeb; Guy Martin; Dorothy Sheridan and her staff in the Special Collections section of the University of Sussex Library, Brighton; Lin and Geff Skippings of (the now renamed) Carlyles' House; John Wagstaff and Edward P. Wilson. Any deficiencies which the volume retains are my responsibility, of course, not theirs.

Carlyle's House

and Other Sketches

Carlyle's House[1]

The bus took me too far. I found myself beyond the embankment[2], saw brown sails at the end of a timber yard. This was how it looked 50 years ago, I suppose. This was how it looked to the Carlyles; but their Row has stucco pillars now, and the fields are stamped out by great municipal buildings of grey brick. I imagine that Carlyle tramped off into muddy lanes, and really got a salt breath from the river, almost at his door. So Chelsea must have been a spacious quarter; with distinct rows of little eighteenth century houses, separated by fields,[3] and with mud banks, and shoals of little boats drawn up on them, running along the river. Mrs Carlyle still speaks of going down to Westminster 'by water'.[4]

But Cheyne Row is spoilt; and Carlyle's house already has the look of something forcibly preserved; it is incongruous now, set between respectable family mansions.

I went in, and a woman speaking broad Scotch showed me over.[5] Why does one do these things? I don't know what I expected to find – something at any rate less cold, and formal.

There were glass cases with specimens of handwriting in the middle of the rooms;[6] otherwise they were bare enough. There were portraits of Mrs Carlyle which seemed to look out quizzically upon the strangers as though she asked what they really found to look at: did they think that her house and her had been like that?[7] Would she have tolerated them for a second?[8]

Her eyes droop in the pictures, and have a peculiar expression, of humour and melancholy lying dormant, which

3

produces this quizzical look that I speak of; at any moment they might flash with passion, or kindle into tenderness. I think that in her life the expression must have been one of mockery for the most part, with a background of pathos; an unhappy face in spite of the brilliant eyes; the late photographs, which exaggerate the hollow of the cheeks, and the length of the upper lip, are horrid.[9] The eyes are the only parts with warmth or depth in them: the rest is granulated skin tight stretched over a skull.

The house is light and spacious; but a silent place, which it needs much imagination to set alive again – one must show it with all her bright little 'contrivances'[10]; and see, somehow, his long gaunt figure, leaning or lying back, pipe in hand; and hear bursts of talk, all in the Scotch accent; and the deep guffaw. Mrs Carlyle, I suppose, sat upright, but very fragile, amused, but critical too – telling her day's narrative, and hitting off some 'admirer' in a phrase or so.[11]

Did one always feel a coldness between them? The only connection the flash of the intellect. I imagine so.

The most natural thing was the garden, with its flags, and the stump of a tree.

Miss Reeves[1]

I met her at dinner last night. She has dark hair, an oval face, with a singularly small mouth: a line is pencilled on her upper lip. She reminds me of the girl whose mother was a snake.[2] There is something of the snake in her. Her eyes are not large, but very bright, hazel colour. She always leans forward, as though to take flight; her whole figure and pose indicating an ardent interested spirit. When she is silent, she thinks – her eyes intent on one spot. But she talks almost incessantly, launching herself with the greatest ease – but says nothing commonplace. Her talk at once flies to social questions; is not dry exposition, but very lucid and vigorous explanation. 'We think...', 'we find' and so on; as though she spoke for the thinking part of the nation. Her vigour struck me most – and the fact that she was not pedantic.

I imagine that her taste and insight are not fine; when she described people she ran into stock phrases, and took rather a cheap view. She seemed determined to be human also; to like people, even though they were stupid.

Her concentration upon one view of life, and her interest in it, seemed to me the most remarkable things about her; with that energy one might get much done, even though one's capacity were not of the finest. She lacks mystery; and the charm people have who withdraw, and don't care to coin their views. One figures her always in flight; so much determined to embrace everything that she fails.

Cambridge

The Darwins' house is a roomy house, built in the 18th century I suppose, overlooking a piece of green.[2] The first things I saw, stepping in from the snow, were a wide hall, with a fire in the middle of it. It is altogether comfortable, and homely. The ornaments, of course, are of the kind that one associates with Dons, and university culture. In the drawing room, the parents' room, there are prints from Holbein drawings, bad portraits of children, indiscriminate rugs, chairs, Venetian glass, Japanese embroideries: the effect is of subdued colour, and incoherence; there is no regular scheme. In short the room is dull.

The children's room revolts against the parents': they like white walls, modern posters, photographs from the old masters. If they could do away with the tradition, I imagine that they would have bare walls, and a stout table; with both ideals I find myself in opposition.

In truth the Darwin temperament deserves some discussion. The parents – Sir George alone was visible – are somewhat obliterated, of course; Sir George is now a very kindly ordinary man, with whom his children are entirely at their ease.[3] It is strange that a man who must have known great men, and who is at work always upon great problems, should have nothing distinguished or remarkable about him. At first one is mildly relieved, and later, one is disappointed. His sensible and humorous remarks, his little anecdotes, and his shrewd judgments, are natural to him; no mask, as one had hoped. He is clearly affectionate, much interested in small events, and satisfied with his position. It is also clear that he has no feeling for beauty, no romance, or mystery in his mind; in short, he is a solid object,[4] filling his place in the world, and all one may ever hope to find in him is a sane judgment, a cheerful temper. The liveliest thing about him is his affection for his children; he is inclined to be peppery, likes punctuality, good manners and tidiness; lectured us, for instance, upon the importance (often overlooked by young ladies) of good shoes. He notices small things; and that, at his age, gives him a certain charm. He is like some elderly but wiry grey terrier, with short legs, and choleric eyes, rather watering at the corners.[5]

His wife (she was in bed) is a big sensible woman; with a trace of American decision: but otherwise merely practical and kindly: coarse I daresay in her view, if one got to know her well. The children almost openly prefer their father.[6]

The children are naturally more interesting. For at their ages, 19 and 24, they are beginning to test their surroundings. They are anxious to get rid of Darwin traditional culture and have a notion that there is a free Bohemian world in London, where exciting people live. This is all to their credit; and indeed they have a certain spirit which one admires. Somehow, however, it applies itself to the wrong things. They aim at beauty, and that requires the surest touch. Gwen[7] tends (this is constructive criticism) to admire vigorous, able, sincere works, which are not beautiful; she attacks the problems of life in the same spirit; and will end in 10 years time by being a strong and sensible woman, plainly clothed; with the works of deserving minor artists in her house.[8] Margaret has not the charm which makes Gwen better than my account of her; a charm arising from the sweetness and competency of her character. She is the eldest of the family. Margaret is much less formed; but has the same determination to find out the truth for herself, and the same lack of any fine power of discrimination.[9] They enjoy things very much, and fancy that this is due to their superior taste; fancy that in riding about the streets of Cambridge they are building up a theory of life. I think I find them content with what seems to me rather obvious; I distrust such violent discontent, and the easy remedies. But I admire much also: only find the Darwin temperament altogether too definite, burly, and industrious. They exhibit the English family life at its best; its humour, tolerance, heartiness, and sound affection.

We also went to tea with James Strachey[10], and one had to consider a very different state of things.

His rooms, though they were lodgings, were dim and discreet;[11] French pastels hung on the walls and there were cases of old books. The three young men – Norton[12], Brooke[13] and James S. – sat in deep chairs; and gazed with soft intent eyes into the fire. Mr Norton knew that he must talk, and he and I spoke laboriously. It was a very difficult duet; the other instruments keeping silent. I should like to account for their silence; but time presses; and I am puzzled.

For the truth is that these young men are evidently respectable; they are not only 'able', but their views seem to me honest, and simple. They lack all padding; so that one has convictions to disagree with, if one disagrees. Yet, we had nothing to say to each other; and I was conscious that not only my remarks but my presence was criticized. They wished for the truth, and doubted whether a woman could speak it or be it. I thought this courageous of them; but unsympathetic. I had to remember that one is not full grown at 21.[14]

At the same time I admired the atmosphere – was it more? – and felt in some respects at ease in it. Why should intellect and character be so barren? It seemed as though the highest efforts of the most civilised people produced a negative result: one could not honestly be anything. I exaggerate however; for I felt, as I have said, the atmosphere; which is only produced by minds and characters which, somehow, affect one pleasantly.

Hampstead

Hampstead is always refreshing. Even on a muddy night there is still some charm; it is so small and quiet. The mud is the mud of country lanes; and the houses, when the lamps flash upon them, are of old red brick, and are sheltered by trees. The Misses Case live on the ridge of the hill, and have a view beneath them on a fine day.[1] Their house is not old, but it has a look of Hampstead; there is something fresh about their furniture, as though the air out here did not stain it. For the rest, the rooms a little shabby; with one or two beautiful pieces of old furniture, and much crockery, such as cultivated and frugal ladies buy, during their summer holidays, in the north of France. The ladies themselves are of a piece with the house; one of them[2], that is, is pale and fresh, and rather shabby, like the furniture, and the other seems to represent the fine and rather austere intellect, tempered by suburban residence, which has filled the rooms with solid works and her Greek archaeology, and hung the walls with photographs from old masters. The look of them is very valiant, humane, and perhaps a little too amiable to be consistent with the very keenest edge of intellect. Both ladies are well over forty.[3]

But there was also another guest, Miss Margaret Davies[4]; and the three together made an harmonious picture. Miss Davies comes of a sterner stock. Her features are sharper, her eyes burn brighter; once she must have had something of the beauty of a delicate Greek head. Now, being also past forty years of age, she has the same look of having passed a strenuous life in toil of some kind for others. Women who have worked but have not married come to have a particular look; refinement, without sex; tending to be austere. Miss Davies, it is clear, has far less tolerance than her friends; and has done what she has done through the force of conviction. She has organised a great co-operative movement in the North. Her eyes have a way of growing dark, as though clouds crossed them, when she is in earnest. I imagine that she might be stern and even bigoted; but that she is also fervent to uphold her lofty views, and has a mind like one of those flint coloured gems upon which the heads of Roman emperors are cut, indelibly.

When three such women meet, however, they generally surprise me by their likeness to schoolgirls. They were at college together,[5] and they like to recall the attitude which was theirs then; they tell humorous and affectionate stories about each other; have the familiarity of a loose, well worn glove. At the same time they drop easily into what I suppose is their shop; they describe the last problem play; they discuss the last development in the fight for the franchise. It is all admirably sane, altruistic, and competent; save for a certain sharpness of edge, it might be the talk of capable members of parliament. I was struck by the conviction with which they spoke; a conviction that justice ought to be done, not to them or their children,[6] but to the whole of womankind. Miss Case tends to be less abstract than Miss Davies, I think; and to have a human being before her always, and not a principle. The elder Miss Case was tenderly laughed at by both of them for her open sentimentality; of which her sister approved more than did her friend.

A Modern Salon

One reads and hears much of the great French salons; and pronounces them always extinct as dodos, although what it is that is extinct, I do not know. It struck me last night, dining with the Morrells, that the effort was certainly in that direction, and if it failed, one would be able to see why.[1] Lady Ottoline has a definite end in view; she is a great lady who has become discontented with her own class, and has found what she wanted in the class of artists, writers, and professional people.[2] For this reason, she approaches them in a definite way; the only thing they have in common is a love of the arts. In return, they see her not as the aristocrat who is shut off from them although they may for a moment come into contact with her, but as a disembodied spirit escaping from her world into a purer air, where she can never take root.

This gives their intercourse a kind of lustre and illusion; they are always conscious that she comes from a distance, with strange colours upon her; and she, that these humbler creatures have yet a vision of the divine.

Her parties have always a certain romance and distinction from the presence of this incongruity. But when one has said that she has this taste for art and artists, one is puzzled to define her gifts any further. Perhaps that says all that there is to be said. At any rate, she seems to devote all her energies to the task, and to be consistently in the same attitude.

Like other people who are passive rather than active, she is very careful and elaborate in her surroundings. It seems that they too play a part.

She is remarkable if not beautiful in her person. She takes the utmost pains to set off her beauty, as though it were a rare object, picked up, with the eye of a connoisseur, in some dusky Florentine back street. It always seems possible that the rich American connoisseurs, who finger her Persian wrapper, and pronounce it 'very good', should go on to criticise her face; 'a fine work – late renaissance, presumably; what modelling in the eyes and brow! but the chin unfortunately is in the weaker style.'

She is curiously passive, even in her expression, and the pallor of her cheeks, the clean cutting of her features, the way she draws her head back and looks at you blankly give her the appearance of a cast from some marble Medusa.[3]

Jews

One wonders how Mrs Loeb became a rich woman. It seems an accident; she might be behind a counter. They had a great gas fire, burning in a florid drawing room.[1] She is a fat Jewess, aged 56 (she tells her age to ingratiate herself) coarsely skinned, with drooping eyes, and tumbled hair. She fawned upon us,[2] flattered us and wheedled us, in a voice that rubbed away the edges of all her words and had a falling cadence. It seemed as though she wished to ingratiate herself with her guests and expected to be kicked by them. Thus at dinner she pressed everyone to eat, and feared, when she saw an empty plate, that the guest was criticising her. Her food, of course, swam in oil and was nasty.

She adjusted her flattery, to suit me, whom she took to be severe and intellectual, and Miss Timothy whom she thought lively and flirtatious.[3] To me she talked of her joy in the open air (she drives regularly in her own carriage), of the 'companionship of books for a lonely woman'[4] (and yet she only dines alone once in the week) of her white bedroom, with its bare walls and open windows. She rallied Miss T. (a chocolate box young woman, a business woman, used to protecting herself) upon the attentions of the hundred men of the orchestra; upon her fat arms; upon the attentions of Syd, her son.[5] What was the truth of the matter, I wonder? I imagine her to be a shrewd woman of business, in the daytime, moving in a circle of city people; 'young people' tickle her coarse palate; she wishes to be popular, and is, perhaps, kind, in her vulgar way, ostentatiously kind to poor relations. The one end she aims at for them, is the society of men and marriage. It seemed very elementary, very little disguised, and very unpleasant.

Divorce Courts

Curiosity took me to the divorce courts, because I had read of a clergyman who seemed to have a bigoted faith, so that he brought religion into contact with his most private life.[1] It seemed substantial: he made his enemy pray with him.

However, I own that it seemed at first as though one were assisting at a torture. The man stood up before us all, and was made to describe his relations with his wife. It was human nature rendering an account to human nature. We sat in judgment. Happily the man was evidently upheld by a kind of formalism[2]; so that the utterances were not so private and therefore painful as they might have been. He vindicated the position of the ideal husband, who must teach, forbear, and help the weaker party.

He spoke the literal truth and enforced it with oaths. He had taken care never to sin: at the same time, he had not any pliancy. His wife had felt dull; he had made a point, in spite of his own scruples, of sending her to the play; he was much occupied with parish duties – always preaching, and overworked. She had fallen into the hands of Miss Lewis, who had revealed to her that she was misunderstood. 'That terrible word "misunderstood"' said the Rector, with some pleasure in finding his troubles conventional. Miss Lewis sat near me. She had a bold, coarse face, strained with the tension of brazening it out before the world. It was old and joyless; but perhaps she was not forty.

Her object had been merely to absorb Mrs Whittingstall entirely; she had not sought money. She had destroyed their marriage by the coarsest blow. Mrs W. was a small, hysterical woman, given to coddling her health, with a waspish temper; yet a lady, and not entirely at ease (perhaps) with her great coarse friend; only Miss Lewis had the will. Mr Whittingstall was in the right, as usual; Mrs W. felt desperate that no one could see what cruelty his right doing implied. It was a nightmare to her. Miss Lewis, and one or two women friends and a hospital nurse,[3] were the only people who saw: the whole male world was against her. No one could doubt the man who remembered every date; was scrupulous enough to own his hot temper – and yet he had tried to control it by prayer and silence; who said outright that he 'adored' his wife; but his character as a clergyman of the Church of England was more to him; who had clearly suffered, and done right, so far as he could see it. One believed him; but he explained the other side as he spoke. He was a man without pity or imagination; a formalist and, perhaps, a selfish man. Moreover, his religion absorbed him. Religion had had much to do with it, I thought. Then he minded what the parishioners thought of him.

She, no doubt, was the less conventional of the two; though the more unjust. He was obviously consoled by the complete vindication of his character, and the consciousness that he had acted rightly and spoken the truth. She will flounder along for a time, one suspects; there will be a disillusionment, when Miss Lewis deserts her for another woman; and then she will come back, and be received with due Christian charity; and some penance will be assigned her, to last her life.

Two things struck me: one was the way he said 'Can you really ask, Sir Edward[4], whether in the course of a married life of 14 years[5], I have ever gone to my wife when she was crying?' It seemed to show one real married life; the kind of humdrum, genuine relationship it is; the human beings so real, giving each other a little comfort, having worn through all disguises and both heavy laden. They suffer.

The other thing was the account he gave of a passionate dispute with his wife, when he raised a crucifix to 'solemnize the scene'; she called it sacrilege, whereupon he took up an earthenware candlestick and fiddled with it, 'as one fiddles with a pen or a pencil.' It was her candlestick, so that he had to drop it when she asked him; a bowl, however, was his, and so he fiddled with that, and she could not make him put it down. It was odd that this should have occupied their mind at such a moment; and that they should have recognised the ownership of the candlestick and bowl.

NOTES

CARLYLE'S HOUSE

1. 24, Cheyne Row, Chelsea. After the death of Thomas Carlyle in 1881, this house, which he had shared with his wife, Jane Welsh Carlyle (d.1866), and which they had first occupied in 1834, was vacated. It was acquired by The Carlyle's House Memorial Trust who opened it, scantily but authentically furnished, in 1895.

2. That is, the Chelsea Embankment, extending from Battersea Bridge to Chelsea Bridge.

3. As she wrote these words, Woolf could well have had in mind her Aunt Anny's childhood memories of Cheyne Row and its surrounding environment: 'There is one part of London which however still seems to me little changed, and this is Cheyne Row, which used to be at the end of all these hawthorn lanes, and Chelsea, whither we used often to go as children, crossing these lanes and fields, and coming by a pond and a narrow street called Paradise Row into the King's Road, and then after a few minutes' walk to Cheyne Row, where Mr and Mrs Carlyle lived to the end of their lives...' Anne Thackeray Ritchie, *Chapters from Some Memoirs* (London: Macmillan, 1894), p. 134.

4. Mrs Carlyle's aquatic journey to Westminster would have begun at the Cadogan Pier (the construction of the Chelsea Embankment began in 1871, five years after Jane Welsh Carlyle's death, and was completed in 1874). I have been unable to pinpoint an example of her using the precise phrase 'by water', but Woolf must surely have had examples like the following in mind: 'We went down the water last night to take tea with the Chaplain of Guy's Hospital...' Jane Carlyle to Miss Margaret Welsh, 15th July 1842, published in James Anthony Froude, ed., *Letters and Memorials of Jane Welsh Carlyle* (London: Longmans, Green, 1883), 3 vols; vol. i, p. 152.

5. Mrs Isabella Strong, Custodian of Carlyle's House from 1895–1917. She was from Kinfauns, near Perth.

6. The many specimens of Carlyle's handwriting on display are listed in the *Illustrated Memorial Volume of the Carlyle's House Purchase Fund Committee with Catalogue of Carlyle's Books, Manuscripts, Pictures and Furniture Exhibited Therein* (1885; rep. London: The Saltire Society, 1995), pp. 98–100.

7. These would have included a copy of a miniature by Kenneth Macleay (1802–78), a watercolour and crayon by Carl Hartmann (1818–57), and an oil painting which has been variously attributed to Samuel Lawrence, Mrs Paulet, Anthony Sterling and Thomas Carrick. See the *Illustrated Memorial Volume*, pp. 89–90.

8. According to the Visitors Book, there were only two other visitors to Carlyle's House on 23rd February 1909, a 'G.C. Hope' of Birkenhead and a 'Kali Hodding' of Salisbury, both of whom signed the book before Woolf.

9. The photographs of Jane Carlyle on display, then and now, are by Robert S. Tait

(1816–97). One, which certainly fits Woolf's description, is dated '28th July 1854'. See also *Illustrated Memorial Volume*, pp. 89–90.

10. This word (and its cognates) was Carlyle's favourite term for Jane's thrifty refurbishment of 24, Cheyne Row. See, for example, Thomas Carlyle's *Reminiscences*, ed. James Anthony Froude (London: Longmans, Green, 1881), 2 vols; vol ii, pp. 179, 231.

11. Jane entertained Carlyle with her 'day's narrative' every evening in the drawing-room when his work was over. There are a number of instances of Jane Carlyle referring to Carlyle's 'admirer[s]'. See, for example, Jane Welsh Carlyle to John Sterling, 1st February 1837: 'I might happen to get myself torn to pieces by the host of my husband's lady admirers…' (*Letters and Memorials of Jane Welsh Carlyle*, i, p. 66.)

MISS REEVES

1. Amber Reeves (1887–1981) had graduated from Newnham College, Cambridge, the previous year, where she had been well known in student political circles. She was the lover of H.G. Wells (1866–1946) at this time.

2. Woolf presumably has in mind the powerfully alluring and snake-like Porphyria in Robert Browning's 'Porphyria's Lover', first published as 'Porphyria' in 1836. While it is not stated in the poem that Porphyria's mother was a snake, her own serpentine qualities are emphasised in various ways. A 'porphyre' is an obsolete word for a snake.

CAMBRIDGE

1. There was no 29th February 1909, of course, so this entry was presumably written on 1st March.

2. Newnham Grange, Cambridge, was built in 1793 for the family of Patrick Beales, a local corn and coal merchant. It was purchased by Sir George Darwin (1845–1912), the second son of Charles Darwin, and Plumian Professor of Astronomy and Experimental Philosophy at Cambridge from 1883 until his death, in 1885. Following its sale by the Darwin family, it became the oldest part of Darwin College, founded in 1964. The 'piece of green' is Queens' Green. For a full account of the house as Woolf would have seen it, see Gwen Raverat, *Period Piece: A Cambridge Childhood* (London: Faber and Faber, 1952), pp. 31–46, and Frances Spalding, *Gwen Raverat: Friends, Family and Affections* (London: Harvill Press, 2001), pp. 47–61.

3. See Gwen Raverat, *Period Piece*, pp. 19–21.

4. This was one of Woolf's preferred terms for the obstructiveness, burdensomeness and tweed-clad predictability of the Victorian patriarchal world.

5. 'As a girl I was apt to consider my elders strangely innocent. Perhaps they really were, though my father was certainly not quite so simple as I thought him then. I remember my intense astonishment when, at a dinner-party, Virginia Stephen

made a slightly double-edged joke, and my father *understood* it! And turned away, shocked! This was, no doubt, chiefly because the joke was made by a young woman.' (Spalding, *Gwen Raverat*, p. 187.)

6. In 1884 Sir George Darwin married Maud (1861–1947), the daughter of Charles Du Puy of Philadelphia. They had two sons (Charles born in 1887 and William born in 1894) and two daughters (Gwen born in 1885 and Margaret born in 1890). See *Period Piece*, pp. 15–17.

7. Gwen Raverat (1885–1957), painter, printmaker and writer. Francis Spalding mentions that 'Gwen still felt nervous when in January 1907 she saw Virginia and Adrian in front of her at the opera in London, and was surprised by their friendliness when eventually they saw her and fell into conversation.' (Spalding, *Gwen Raverat*, p. 117.) She married Jacques Raverat in 1911.

8. Gwen Raverat, in fact, very soon went on to the Slade and by the autumn of 1909 she was 'painting, as well as drawing and woodcutting… She had begun to see more of the Stephen family, dining with Virginia and Adrian at their home in Fitzroy Square and attending meetings of the Friday Club which Vanessa had started a couple of years before.' (Spalding, *Gwen Raverat*, p. 163.)

9. She went on to marry Geoffrey Keynes (1887–1982), surgeon and Blake scholar, who in 1913 would save Woolf's life after she took an overdose.

10. James Strachey (1887–1967) was then at Trinity College, Cambridge. He was the younger brother of Lytton Strachey. James and his wife Alix, whom he married in 1920, went on to achieve distinction as the first translators of Freud's work into English and became psychoanalysts in their own right. For something of the atmosphere Woolf must have encountered, see Keith Hale, ed., *Friends and Apostles: The Correspondence of Rupert Brooke and James Strachey, 1905–1914* (New Haven and London: Yale University Press, 1998), pp. 49–90.

11. This passage, from 'His rooms' to 'honestly be anything', was quoted by Woolf in 'Old Bloomsbury', a talk she gave to the Memoir Club either in late 1921 or early 1922. Woolf said at the time she was quoting from a 'diary which I kept intermittently for a month or two in the year 1909… I am describing a tea-party in James Strachey's rooms at Cambridge.' In 'Old Bloomsbury', Woolf puts the first sentence in the present tense and transposes 'dim' and 'discreet' as well as making a number of other minor changes to the text. See Virginia Woolf, *Moments of Being*, ed. Jeanne Schulkind. Introduced and revised by Hermione Lee (London: Pimlico, 2002), pp. 53–55.

12. The mathematician H. T. J. Norton (1886–1937).

13. Woolf had known the poet Rupert Brooke (1887–1915) 'slightly as a child' (Lee, p. 292), and in the summer of 1911 she would bathe naked in the moonlight with him, once, at Grantchester (Lee, p. 295). By 1909, James Strachey was 'hopelessly in love' with Brooke (Lee, p. 293).

14. This sentence is not quoted in 'Old Bloomsbury'.

HAMPSTEAD

1. Their address was 5, Windmill Hill, Hampstead.

2. Emphie (Euphemia) Case.

3. Janet Case (1862–1937) was then aged forty-seven, twenty years Woolf's senior. She had first tutored Woolf in Greek in 1902–3.

4. Margaret Llewelyn Davies (1861–1944) was General Secretary of the Women's Co-operative Guild from 1889 to 1922.

5. All three women had been undergraduates at Girton College, Cambridge.

6. In fact, none of the three women had any children.

A MODERN SALON

1. 'In the spring of 1907, [Lady Ottoline Morrell (1873–1938)] began issuing invitations to her famous "Thursdays". A few close friends were invited to dinner; slight acquaintances were told to come later and to dress as informally as they liked. Watching the writers and painters and musicians crowding into the drawing-room, planning who could be of most use to each of them, Ottoline felt that she had begun to discover her vocation at last. She could enhance the lives of people she admired.' Miranda Seymour, *Ottoline Morrell: Life on the Grand Scale* (London: Hodder and Stoughton, 1992), p. 75. 'Once a week,' Mary Agnes Hamilton recalled in 1944 of a period just after 1909, Lady Ottoline Morrell '…used to be at home, and at [44] Bedford Square, in the great, double room on the first floor, with its superb fires, its deliciously soft chairs, its interesting modern pictures on the walls, and its masses of glorious flowers arranged with the most loving cunning, the rebels gathered, for coffee and cigarettes and talk.' *Remembering My Good Friends* (London: Jonathan Cape, 1944), p. 74.

2. Woolf draws on this passage from 'Lady Ottoline… is a great lady' to the end of this sketch in 'Old Bloomsbury' (*Moments of Being*, pp. 59–60), but this original, uncut version is more cutting.

3. See Woolf's letter to Madge Vaughan of May 1909: 'We have just got to know a wonderful Lady Ottoline Morrell, who has the head of a Medusa; but she is very simple and innocent in spite of it, and worships the arts,' *Letters*, i, p. 395. See also Lee, p. 276, for Woolf's falseness towards Lady Ottoline.

JEWS

1. The Loebs lived at 4, Lancaster Gate, London.

2. It is likely that Woolf was accompanied by her brother Adrian Stephen and their mutual friend Saxon Sydney-Turner.

3. Miriam Jane Timothy (1879–1950) was then a harpist of great prominence. She entered the Royal College of Music at the age of fourteen and went on to become, among other things, the only woman in Queen Victoria's private band, having been appointed to it in January 1900; she continued in this role when it became King

Edward VII's private band in 1901, and when it became King George V's band in 1910. In a letter to Percy Pitt of 13th January 1914, Hans Richter, writing from Germany, confided: 'I often see myself with my English orchestra [the London Symphony Orchestra]… The ever-present and beautiful Miss Timothy, as excellent on the harp as on the lute…' Christopher Fifield, *True Artist and True Friend: A Biography of Hans Richter* (Oxford: Clarendon Press, 1993), p. 446; see also p. 449. According to her pupil, Marie Goossens, 'Miriam Timothy was renowned as a harpist and a beautiful woman.' Marie Goossens, *Life on a Harp String* (London: Thorne, 1987), p. 32. Timothy taught at the RCM from 1910 to 1919.

4. Her husband had died in the mid-1890s, when her son, Sydney, was in his last year at Harrow.

5. Sydney J. Loeb (1877–1964), was a stockbroker and passionate Wagnerian.

DIVORCE COURTS

1. The Revd Herbert Oakes Fearnley-Whittingstall was born on 15th March 1859 and died on 4th November 1949. He was educated at Eton and New College, Oxford. In 1891 he married Alice Wethered (1866–1945). Fearnley-Whittingstall had been Rector of Chalfont St Giles in Buckinghamshire since 1902.

2. Woolf is using this word in its theological sense: 'The basing of ethics on the form of the moral law without regard to intention or consequences' (*OED*).

3. In *The Times* report of 4th November 1909 (p. 3), they are named as 'Miss Greenwood, Nurse Yendell, and Miss Gallwey'.

4. Mrs Fearnley-Whittingstall's counsel.

5. This must be Woolf's mistake; they had been married 18 years in 1909.

COMMENTARY

CARLYLE'S HOUSE

Most readers of this first sketch will be surprised to learn that Woolf's excursion to Carlyle's House on 23rd February 1909 was not her first such outing. 'I don't know what I expected to find – something at any rate less cold, and formal,' Woolf writes here, but she must have had a pretty good idea of what she would come across since she had visited the house twice before, once with her father, on 29th January 1897,[1] and once with her sister and Hester Ritchie, on 29th March 1898.[2] Of course, Woolf may mean that she didn't know what *changes* she might 'find', but, all the same, her description of the house has all the feel and resonance of a first encounter. (Incidentally, the 'woman speaking broad Scotch' who acted as Woolf's cicerone in 1909 was the same woman who had been her guide in 1897 and 1898, but Woolf's apparent failure to recognise Mrs Strong, the Custodian of Carlyle's House, is perhaps more understandable.)

Woolf's third visit to Carlyle's House took place six days after Lytton Strachey had proposed to her and three days after the idea had been abandoned. 'She declared she was not in love with me, and I observed finally that I would not marry

1. 'After Lunch father took me to see Carlyles house in Chelsea – Walked there – Went over the house, with an intelligent old woman who knew father and everything about him – We saw the drawing room, and dining room, and C's sound proof room, with double walls – His writing table, and his pens, and scraps of his manuscripts – Pictures of him and her everywhere.' (*A Passionate Apprentice*, p. 24.)
2. We know this from the Carlyle's House Visitors Book. Hester Ritchie, then aged twenty, was the daughter of Woolf's aunt, Anne Isabella Ritchie, née Thackeray. Woolf visited the house for at least a fourth time on 16th March 1931 when preparing her essay on 'Great Men's Houses', *Good Housekeeping*, 21, No.1 (March 1932), pp. 10–11; 102–3. Rep. in Virginia Woolf, *The London Scene* (London: The Hogarth Press, 1982), pp. 23–9.

her. So things have simply reverted,' Strachey told his friend Leonard Woolf.[3] But this was by no means the end of the matter for Virginia Stephen. Becoming Mrs Strachey might have been out of the question, '[b]ut she did want to be married; she was twenty-seven years old, tired of spinsterhood, very tired of living with Adrian and very fond of Lytton. She needed a husband whose mind she could respect; she valued intellectual eminence above everything and in this respect no rival had yet appeared.'[4]

Woolf began her 1904 essay on 'Haworth', the family home of the Brontës, by wondering 'whether pilgrimages to the shrines of famous men ought not to be condemned as sentimental journeys. It is better to read Carlyle in your own study chair than to visit the sound-proof room and pore over the manuscripts at Chelsea.'[5] Yet the main reason why she visited Carlyle's House in February 1909 was almost certainly to reacquaint herself with the spirit of the place in just such a manner as she prepared to review *The Love Letters of Thomas Carlyle and Jane Welsh* for the *TLS*. But it is just possible that her third expedition to Cheyne Row was also a kind of 'sentimental journey'. It has been suggested that one of Woolf's chief motives for wishing to marry Strachey was to break free from the shadow of Leslie Stephen (even if, in doing so, she would be choosing the one suitor who would go on to resemble her father the most, especially after the rangy Strachey grew an impressive High-Victorian beard in 1911). Alternatively, Woolf's journey to Carlyle's House may have been an attempt to reach back to her father – and mother – at a

3. Holroyd, *Lytton Strachey*, p. 202.
4. Bell, i, p. 141.
5. Andrew McNeillie, ed., *The Essays of Virginia Woolf* (London: Hogarth Press, 1986), i, pp. 5–9. Quotation from p. 5. Hereafter, *Essays*. See also pp. 54–8 for Woolf's essay based on *The Letters and Memorials of Jane Welsh Carlyle* (2nd August 1905).

time of emotional upset. By visiting the home of one of the most celebrated couples of the nineteenth century, a man and wife, furthermore, whose turbulent and well-documented domesticity bore at least some resemblance to her own parents' 'destructive and dark relationship'[6], Woolf may in some sense have felt she was getting as close as she could to her own lost home. As Andrew McNeillie has observed, 'The Carlyles' marriage was a topic with which the Stephen family were perhaps more familiar than most: "I was not as bad as Carlyle, was I?" being part of the rhetoric on Leslie Stephen's remorseful lips after his own wife's death'[7] in 1895. The previous day, 22nd February 1909, had been the fifth anniversary of her father's death.

Moreover, in a *very* loose sense, Carlyle's House was Leslie Stephen's house, in that he had been Chairman of the Carlyle's House Purchase Fund Committee in 1894–5.[8] As Woolf wandered round the house, she would have recalled her first visit there with her father, called to mind his leading role in the purchase of the property, and seen a photograph of Carlyle's Eightieth Birthday Tribute, signed by, among others, George Eliot, Charles Darwin, Robert Browning, Tennyson and Leslie Stephen. Although her feelings for her father were deeply ambivalent and would remain so throughout her life, in 1909 she still held Leslie Stephen in awe.

Carlyle and Stephen had been moderately warm friends and Stephen had written the entry on the 'Sage of Chelsea' in the *Dictionary of National Biography*, but Carlyle had been a much closer friend of Woolf's fraternal uncle, Sir James Fitzjames Stephen (1829–94). He appointed J.F. Stephen to be

6. Lee, p. 94.
7. *Essays*, i, p. 261.
8. The CHPFC Minute Book is kept at Carlyles' House.

an executor of his will, and when he died in 1881, Carlyle bequeathed his friend one of his most precious possessions: his writing desk. Overall, there were a number of connections between the two families, and especially between Leslie and Julia Stephen and Thomas and Jane Carlyle, and it is hard to resist musing on how many of them were active in Woolf's mind and tugging at her heart as she entered Carlyle's House on 23rd February. In this respect it is particularly striking that the word Woolf uses to describe Jane Welsh Carlyle's facial skin in 'Carlyle's House' is 'granulated': '...the rest is granulated skin tight stretched over a skull.' There are only two other uses of this unusual word in Woolf's entire oeuvre and one of them is when Woolf describes the facial skin of her dead mother in her 'Sketch of the Past': 'Whenever I touch cold iron the feeling comes back to me – the feeling of my mother's face, iron cold, and granulated.'[9]

However, there is another context for Woolf's visit to Carlyle's House which is rather less speculative. Lee has argued, persuasively, that Woolf's review of the Carlyles' *Love Letters* 'can plausibly be read as a continuation of [Woolf and Strachey's] conversation about marriage. The Carlyles' intellectual relationship in the period of their courtship is eloquently described: "It was his intellect that she admired, and it was her intellect that she would have him admire... He took her genius very seriously, and did his best to draw up a programme for the cultivation of it." '[10] And it is possible to extend Lee's convincing analogy even further. For instance, when Woolf writes of Carlyle and Jane Welsh a little further on in her review: 'Even though they were never to speak of love, they find that they have much else to speak of, and

9. 'Sketch of the Past', *Moments of Being*, p. 102.
10. Lee, p. 260.

gradually their first vague raptures give way to a more definite relationship; they discover that they are remarkable people – "two originals for certain… it is very kind in Fortune to have brought us together; otherwise we might have gone on single-handed to the end of time",[11] we could well be eavesdropping on Woolf's hopes for what the future would hold for Strachey and herself. If so, her hopes were largely realised. And was Woolf taking a quick mental glance at the spare and lanky Strachey when she wrote, in her 1909 journal sketch, of Carlyle's 'long gaunt figure, leaning or lying back' of an evening at 24, Cheyne Row? Carlyle's 'Scotch accent' and 'deep guffaw', of course, are not remotely Lytton Stracheyan.

* * *

MISS REEVES

The only glimpse we have had of Amber Reeves in Woolf's writings up until now has been a brief sighting of her in a letter to Lytton Strachey of 28th April 1908, in which Woolf recalls seeing 'Rupert Brooke once, leaning over the gallery at Newnham, in midst of Miss Reeves and the Fabians.'[12]

By 1909, Reeves was an extremely energetic Fabian as well as a charismatic and much talked-about young woman of great passion and intellect.[13] Born in Christchurch, New Zealand, on 1st July 1887, she went up to Newnham College, Cambridge, in October 1905. Both her parents were Fabians and her father had been in England as the New Zealand

11. *Essays*, i, p. 258.
12. *Letters*, i, p. 328.
13. For the following information about Amber Reeves I am largely indebted to Ruth Fry, *Maud and Amber: A New Zealand Mother and Daughter and the Women's Cause 1865 to 1981* (Christchurch, New Zealand: Canterbury University Press, 1992). Page references to quotations from this book are embodied in the text.

Agent-General since 1896. His daughter had been educated at Kensington High School for Girls and at a finishing-school in Lausanne.

Reeves made an immediate impact at Cambridge: to a fellow-student, she was 'intellect personified' (p. 46). But she also acquired a different kind of reputation, and it was eventually rumoured that she had disappeared to Paris for the weekend with the writer, one-man think-tank and Fabian family friend, H.G. Wells. 'The authorities at Cambridge were not a little worried by Amber's flaunting of the rules and conventions, and the students were agog… While the dons were busy trying to hush up the story, her image among the students soared. "She became more daring than anyone else we knew," one of them wrote. "We thought of her with awe." ' (p. 50). Wells described the Amber Reeves of this period as 'a girl of brilliant and precocious promise. She had a sharp, bright, Levantine face under a shock of very fine abundant black hair, a slender, nimble body very much alive, and a quick greedy mind. She became my adherent and a great propagandist of Wellsianism at Newnham College.'[14]

Paul Delany, in *The Neo-pagans*, describes the sexually precocious 'eye-catcher' throwing herself into the arms of Wells in the spring of 1908 and bedding the Fabian heavy-weight at Newnham. Their lovemaking on this occasion had to be restricted 'because H.G. had failed to stop at a chemist first' but their relationship soon developed into a full-blooded affair.[15]

By the summer of 1908, following Reeves' success in her

14. G.P. Wells, ed., *H.G. Wells in Love: Postscript to an Experiment in Autobiography* (London: Faber and Faber, 1984), p. 73. For Wells's account of his relationship with Reeves, see pp. 73–86.
15. Paul Delany, *The Neo-pagans: Rupert Brooke and the Ordeal of Love* (New York: The Free Press, 1987), pp. 35–6.

final examinations, the Fabian leader Beatrice Webb was describing her as 'the brilliant Amber Reeves, the double first Moral Tripos, an amazingly vital person and I suppose very clever, but a terrible little pagan – vain, egotistical, and careless of other people's happiness... A somewhat dangerous friendship is springing up between her and H.G. Wells... if Amber were my child I should be anxious.'[16]

Mrs Webb's fears were well founded and 'Miss Reeves' eventually became pregnant by Wells in the spring of 1909. She bore his child on 31st December 1909, having married Rivers Blanco White, who had fallen in love with her at Cambridge, on 7th May. Amber Blanco White went on to write a number of novels and works of non-fiction, contributed regularly and extensively to periodicals, and worked for the women's, Labour and Fabian movements for most of the rest of her life (though she did vote Tory in the 1970 General Election). For thirty-seven years she tutored at Morley College in London, where Woolf herself had taught from 1905 to 1907. She died in 1981.

A few months after this piece was written, in August 1909, Strachey characterised Woolf as 'young, wild, inquisitive, discontented, and longing to be in love',[17] and perhaps this was why she found the alluring Reeves worth writing about. Certainly, she seems almost envious of Reeves' social ease and intellectual lucidity. When Woolf contrasts Reeves' looks and intellectual glamour with 'the charm people have who withdraw, and don't care to coin their views', she obviously has herself in mind; but is her tone self-possessed, haughty, or inflected with pathos?

16. Quoted in Ruth Fry, *Maud and Amber*, p. 51.
17. Quoted in Frederic Spotts, *Letters of Leonard Woolf* (London: Weidenfeld and Nicolson, 1989), p. 149.

* * *

CAMBRIDGE

Immediately before telling Strachey about spotting Brooke among the Fabians at Newnham (see the 'Miss Reeves' section above), Woolf professed to having been deeply impressed by Strachey's account of staying in a hotel in Wiltshire with his brother James, John Maynard Keynes, G.E. Moore, Rupert Brooke and other young Cambridge men: 'You terrify me with your congregations of intellect upon Salisbury plain. My reverence for clever young men affects me with a kind of mental palsy. I really cannot conceive what the united minds of all those you name produced by way of talk. Did you – but I can't begin to consider it even.' It is quite possible that Woolf is being ironic here, and less than a year later any 'reverence' for young Cambridge had most definitely cooled.

In 'Cambridge', Woolf describes a visit she made to James Strachey's rooms, where she also came across Rupert Brooke, whom she knew slightly, and the noted mathematician H. T. J. Norton, whom she first met in 1908. Woolf tells us that she had felt put out by the silence and self-centredness of Strachey and Brooke as she'd battled to make conversation with Norton, and many years later, in the talk she gave on 'Old Bloomsbury', Woolf looked back on this occasion as a watershed. She quotes an extract from this journal (from 'His rooms' to 'honestly be anything') and then analyses what she's written:

'There is a great change there from what I should have written two or three years earlier. In part, of course, the change was due to circumstances; I lived alone with Adrian now in Fitzroy Square; and we were the most incompatible of people. We drove each other perpetually into frenzies of irritation or into the depths of gloom... True, we still had Thursday evenings as before. But they were always strained and often ended in dismal failure. Adrian stalked off to his room, I to mine, in complete silence. But there was more in it than that. What it was I was not altogether certain... Those long sittings, those long silences, those long arguments – they still went on in Fitzroy Square as they had done in Gordon Square. But now I found them of the most perplexing nature. They still excited me much more than any men I met with in the outer world of dinners and dance – and yet I was, dared I say it or think it even? – intolerably bored. Why, I asked, had we nothing to say to each other? Why were the most gifted of people also the most barren? Why were the most stimulating of friendships also the most deadening? Why was it all so negative? Why did these young men make one feel that one could not honestly be anything? The answer to all my questions was, obviously... that there was no physical attraction between us.

The society of buggers has many advantages – if you are a woman. It is simple, it is honest, it makes one feel... in some respects at one's ease. But it has this drawback – with buggers one cannot, as nurses say, show off. Something is always suppressed, held down. Yet this showing off, which is not copulating, necessarily, nor altogether being in love, is one of the great delights, one of the chief necessities of life. Only then does all effort cease; one ceases to be honest, one ceases to be clever. One fizzes up into some absurd delightful effervescence of soda water or champagne through which one sees the world tinged with all the colours of the rainbow. It is significant of what I had come to desire that I went straight – on almost the next page of my diary indeed – from the dim and discreet rooms of James Strachey at Cambridge to dine with Ottoline Morrell at Bedford Square. Her rooms, I noted without drawing any inferences, seemed to me instantly full of "lustre and illusion".'[18]

Prior to calling on James Strachey, Woolf had paid a visit to Newnham Grange, the Cambridge home of Sir George Darwin and his family. Sir Leslie Stephen and Sir George Darwin had been good friends, and Woolf had continued to call on the Darwins while Thoby was up at Cambridge and after his death in 1906. Her visit provides the opportunity for her to knock the Victorians and their tastes, but it is interesting too that she also mentions the strengths of the Victorian family: 'They exhibit the English family life at its best; its humour, tolerance, heartiness, and sound affection.'

* * *

HAMPSTEAD

In 'Old Bloomsbury', Woolf gives the impression that her 1909 diary moves straight from James Strachey's rooms in Cambridge to Lady Ottoline Morrell's London salon, but it doesn't. Before her evening at 44, Bedford Square, Woolf travels north to the Hampstead home of Janet Case and her sister. Woolf had a number of important friendships with older women, such as Violet Dickinson, Kitty Maxse and Madge Vaughan, and her friendship with Janet Case (1862–1937) was one of the more significant of these: she is named as one of the friends who Woolf said had 'helped [her] in ways too various to specify' in the preface to *Orlando* (1928). Case tutored

18. *Moments of Being*, p. 54–5.

Woolf in Greek from 1902–3, and Woolf wrote a portrait of her in her 1903 journal:

> 'When I first saw her one afternoon in the drawing room, she seemed to me exactly what I had expected – tall, classical looking, masterfull [*sic*]. But I was bored at being taught, & for some time, only did just what was asked from me, & hardly looked up from my book – that is at my teacher. But she was worth looking at. She had fine bright eyes – a curved nose, the teeth too prominent indeed – but her whole aspect was vigorous & wholesome. She taught well too… But I am sorry to say… that she did not at first attract me. She was too cheerful & muscular. She made me feel "contracdictious" as the nurses used to say… She talked on many subjects; & on all she showed herself possessed of clear strong views, & more than this she had the rare gift of seeing the other side; she had too, I think, a fine human sympathy which I had reason, once or twice to test…'[19]

Woolf penned this sketch when she thought her lessons with Janet Case had come to an end, but she took them up again later in 1903 and the two women remained friends from then on. When Janet Case died in 1937, Woolf wrote an unsigned obituary for *The Times*, and in her diary she paid tribute to the 'visionary part' Case had played in her life.[20]

Woolf also remained friendly with Margaret Llewelyn Davies for many years after 1909. In 1913, at her suggestion, the Woolfs travelled to Newcastle upon Tyne to attend the Women's Co-operative Guild annual conference. In her vivid 'Introductory

19. *A Passionate Apprentice*, pp. 182–4.
20. Anne Olivier Bell, ed., *The Diary of Virginia Woolf (Volume v: 1936–1941)* (London: The Hogarth Press, 1984), p. 103.

Letter to Margaret Llewelyn Davies' (1930), Woolf recalls the conference in great detail and conjures up other aspects of the WCG movement, especially the staff and activities of its Hampstead headquarters, before concluding her essay: 'Have not you and Lilian Harris [the life-long partner of Margaret Llewelyn Davies] given your best years – but hush! you will not let me finish that sentence and therefore, with the old messages of friendship and admiration, I will make an end.'[21]

* * *

A Modern Salon

Woolf concluded her 'Old Bloomsbury' talk with a description of her first dinner party at the 44, Bedford Square home of Lady Ottoline Morrell (1873–1938). She had first met Lady Ottoline towards the end of the previous year and the aristocratic hostess wrote to Woolf, asking if she would be her friend, in January 1909.[22] As Hermione Lee writes:

> 'Ottoline's appearance was legendarily idiosyncratic. She spoke in a weird, nasal, cooing, sing-song drawl. Her amazing looks were at once sexy and grotesque: she was very tall, with a huge head of copper-coloured hair, turquoise eyes and great beaky features. She wore fantastical highly-coloured clothes and hats with great style and bravado, and had pronounced tastes in interior decoration.'[23]

21. Co-operative Working Women, *Life As We Have Known It,* ed. Margaret Llewelyn Davies (London: Hogarth Press, 1931), p. xxxix. In her thirty-two years in office, Margaret Llewelyn Davies never once took a salary.
22. *Letters*, i, p. 381.
23. Lee, p. 275.

Lady Ottoline was thirty-six at the time of Woolf's description of her salon and, as is all too clear, Woolf was in many ways unsympathetic towards her extraordinary new friend. In later years Woolf would come to regret the hurtful things she had thought and said of her around this time. 'In 1932, reading Ottoline's accounts of difficult visits to Fitzroy Square, Virginia was bitterly and vividly reminded of her own ghost... Did Ottoline know how unhappy she was then, how much she hated those evenings, how much loneliness and terror she felt? And how when Adrian finally banged shut the door on Lytton or Saxon at two or three o'clock in the morning, she used to stumble off to bed in despair?'[24]

'When the history of Bloomsbury is written,' Woolf remarked towards the end of her 'Old Bloomsbury' talk, '...there will have to be a chapter... devoted to Ottoline... I find from my diary that I dined with her on March the 30th 1909 – I think for the first time...' She then describes attending one of Ottoline's Thursday evenings with Rupert Brooke (it's not clear if she is referring to a previous occasion or the same one she describes in this journal) which she pictures as an 'extraordinary whirlpool where such odd sticks and straws were brought momentarily together'. A few lines further on, Woolf quotes from the 1909 notebook, from 'Lady Ottoline... is a great lady' to 'She is curiously passive', before adding:

'When indeed one remembers that drawing room full of people, the pale yellows and pinks of the brocades, the Italian chairs, the Persian rugs, the embroideries, the tassels, the scent, the pomegranates, the pugs, the pot-pourri and

24. Lee, p. 277. Saxon Sydney-Turner (1880–1962) had been at Cambridge with Thoby, Lytton Strachey and Clive Bell.

Ottoline bearing down upon one from afar in her white shawl with the great scarlet flowers on it and sweeping one away out of the large room and the crowd into a little room with her alone, where she plied one with questions that were so intimate and so intense, about life and one's friends, and made one sign one's name in a little scented book... I think my excitement may be excused.'[25]

* * *

JEWS

There is now a gap of seven months before the final entry in the diary, a double header entitled 'Jews and Divorce Courts' which has been split into two separate sketches in this edition as it is quite clear that Woolf's portmanteau title is purely functional: indeed, Woolf herself separates 'Jews and Divorce Courts' with a clear division in her notebook.

Between dining with Ottoline Morrell at the end of March and writing 'Jews and Divorce Courts' on 3rd November, Woolf kept herself remarkably busy. In April she was left the large sum of £2,500 on the death of her Aunt Caroline Stephen (Vanessa and Adrian were only bequeathed £100 each) and that month she visited Italy with Vanessa and Clive Bell, but was unhappy and came home alone. 'It was rather melancholy,' Vanessa wrote to a friend, 'to see her start off on that long journey alone leaving us together here! Of course I am sometimes impressed by the pathos of her position & I have been so more here than usual. I think she would like very much to marry & certainly she would like much better to marry Lytton than anyone else. It is difficult living with Adrian who does not appreciate her & to live with him till the

25. *Moments of Being*, pp. 59–60.

end of their days is a melancholy prospect.'[26] That May, in Cambridge, she turned down another suitor, Hilton Young, when he proposed to her in a punt.

We get a good sense of the energy Woolf expended in mid-1909, both physical and emotional, in Hermione Lee's digest of Adrian Stephen's summer diary. He recorded:

'some adventurous outings, like a fancy-dress party at the Botanical Gardens when Virginia went dressed as Cleopatra... There were more conventional outings to plays, operas and concerts: *Aida*, *Electra*, Lillian Nordica at the Queen's Hall, *Orpheus and Eurydice* at Drury Lane, an Arnold Bennett play, Wagner operas, and the première of Ethel Smyth's *The Wreckers*... There were expeditions to the zoo, to Speakers' Corner, to the Friday Club shows, for ices at Buzzards. Virginia was busy – writing, teaching, taking German lessons, sitting for her portrait, going to soirées, dinners and entertainments, parties, weekends in the country and holidays in Europe, and playing host at the new Fitzroy Square "Thursday evenings"...

But underneath... Woolf was still extremely vulnerable. She missed Thoby intensely. She walked about London "engaged with my anguish... alone; fighting something alone." '[27]

In August 1909 Woolf visited Bayreuth with Adrian and Saxon Sydney-Turner. Soon after returning from Germany, she shot off to Studland in Dorset to be near Vanessa, and the year came to a close with her suddenly deciding, during a walk in Regent's Park on 24th December, to spend Christmas alone

26. Quoted in Bell, i, p. 144.
27. Lee, pp. 239–40. See also *Essays*, i, 269–72, 288–93.

in Cornwall. Nowhere is the contrast between the restless, eventful, even exciting social life Woolf led in 1909 and her more muted inner world more stark than in the discrepancy between the lively tone of her letters in 1909 – especially the ones from Bayreuth – and the veiled voice of this private journal.

A risky and protracted flirtation with Clive Bell, which had developed after the birth of Julian, was still ongoing in 1909 and was to last for about another year, but her ongoing and far more serious struggle with her novel was to last much longer than that: it would eventually appear as *The Voyage Out* in 1915. 'I was unhappy that summer,' Woolf later recalled, 'and bitter in all my judgements.'[28] On one occasion she caught the eye of a stranger during a Hans Richter concert at the Queen's Hall. He 'thought she looked so "lonely and sad" that he followed her home and wrote to her, offering her a ticket for a play. She sat next to him (the play was Galsworthy's *Strife*) but when he wrote again she let it drop.'[29]

Of the seven sketches in this journal, Woolf's 'bitter[ness]' is most conspicuous in 'Jews'. Here, the reader must confront both a liberated and independent-minded young woman refusing to play the role of desirable trophy she feels her affluent hostess wants her to be, a young woman who would blossom, in time, into one of the most influential writers and feminists of the twentieth century, and also a bigot, enslaved to an age-old form of prejudice. Apart from the odd passing slur in her earlier journals,[30] 'Jews', from now on, will bear the doubtful distinction of being Woolf's first significant anti-Semitic smear.

'The whirl of the London season is upon us,' Woolf wrote to

28. Quoted in Bell, i, p. 143.
29. Lee, p. 241.
30. See *A Passionate Apprentice*, pp. 224, 259, 261.

Lytton Strachey on 4th June 1909. '...I am penetrating into the most mysterious places. There is a Jewess who spends 50 guineas on a hat, and wishes to meet me, not that we may exchange views on that subject, I imagine. We see her at the opera, where she displays a wonderful arm upon the ledge of her box. Then, upstairs we meet Charlie Sanger, and Saxon and the great Mr Loeb who has the finest collection of operatic photographs and autographs in Europe.'[31]

The 'Jewess' in question was almost certainly Mrs Annie Loeb, and 'Mr Loeb' her son Sydney J. Loeb. Annie Loeb, née Sewill, (1854-1939) was the widow of Siegmund Loeb (1841-c.95), a German Jew from Frankfurt who had come to England to pursue his business interests in the City of London. By 1881 he was a naturalised British subject. Annie Loeb had been born in Liverpool and is remembered fondly by her granddaughter, Sylvia Loeb, as 'a lady of leisure, large, fat and gregarious'.[32]

Sydney J. Loeb (1877-1964), in 1909, was a successful stockbroker and a long-standing Wagnerian of unquenchable fervour - indeed, it is highly likely that Woolf, Adrian and Saxon Sydney-Turner would have bumped into this dedicated aficionado of the composer during their August holiday in Bayreuth, as Loeb attended the festival without fail. In 1912 he married the youngest daughter of the great Wagnerian conductor Hans Richter and went on to become one of the most consummate Wagnerians of his generation. He clearly made a deep impression on Richter. Writing to a friend who had expressed an objection to Loeb on the grounds of his race, 'Richter defended his future son-in-law against

31. *Letters*, i, p. 398. In their footnote, Nigel Nicolson and Joanne Trautmann misidentify 'Mr Loeb' as 'James Loeb (1867-1933), the American banker, who founded the Institute of Musical Art in New York and the Loeb Classical Library'.
32. In conversation with Christopher Fifield.

his friend's antipathy towards him. Loeb was, he said, a responsible and honourable man whom he liked very much.'[33]

Loeb was also an expert on Elgar, and his close friendship with August Jaeger (1860–1909), the inspiration behind Elgar's *Nimrod* variation and the composer's great protector and encourager, 'was to prove greatly supportive' to Jaeger in his declining years.[34] Indeed, the most detailed account of Sydney Loeb currently available is provided by Jaeger's biographer:

'Loeb's German Jewish forbears had come to England, like the Jaegers, to escape the Bismarck factor… Sydney received a classic English education at Harrow, where he was a near contemporary of Winston Churchill, and grew up to become a connoisseur of the arts and music. His extant engagement diaries for the years from 1901 to 1920 [they have been checked for the period around 1909 and they contain no references to Woolf] tell of close acquaintance, not only with London's musical life, but with the intellectual and political world also; he attended Fabian lectures and suffragette meetings, and several times sought out, and recorded, the conversation of Bernard Shaw. But music came first. He attended all kinds of orchestral and chamber concerts and song recitals, and became a discriminating judge of singers… Sustained by a comfortable and apparently undemanding Stock Exchange career and blessed with a gregarious and generous nature, Loeb led a busy social life… [He] took up photography as

33. Fifield, *True Artist and True Friend*, p. 439.
34. Kevin Allen, *August Jaeger: Portrait of Nimrod: A Life in Letters and Other Writings* (Aldershot: Ashgate, 2000), p. 178.

a hobby and became an enthusiastic and accomplished practitioner, snapping his idols in an extensive series of refreshingly informal photographs, subsequently mounted in handsome volumes. But his greatest love was for opera... Loeb's diaries show that he attended virtually every Wagner performance in London for a period of 19 years, clocking up 50 *Mastersingers* and 63 *Tristans*, together with many *Ring* cycles...'[35]

It is important to establish the substance, seriousness and kindness of Loeb, because this is the same 'Mr Loeb' who would stop Leonard and Virginia Woolf in Hyde Park one day in the mid-1920s and receive the sharp end of her tongue. On 1st June 1925 Woolf wrote in her diary:

'It is a sunny fitful day, & standing in Hyde Park to listen to the socialists, that furtive Jew, Loeb, who dogs my life at intervals of 10 years, touched us on the shoulder, & took 2 photographs of us, measuring his distance with a black tape, provided by his wife. He usually tells people to hold one end next their hearts: but this is a joke. He had been hanging around Covent Garden to photograph singers & had lunched at 2.30. I asked if he were a professional, which hurt his pride: he owned to taking great interest in it, & said he had a large collection.'[36]

35. Allen, *August Jaeger*, pp. 178–9. Allen includes a good many letters from Jaeger to Loeb, and provides details of Loeb's 'thoughtful kindness' (p. 267) towards Jaeger in the last months of his life. See in particular Chapter 14, '1909: "I can no more..."', especially pp. 264–70. Jaeger died of tuberculosis on 18th May 1909.
36. Anne Olivier Bell, ed. *The Diary of Virginia Woolf (Volume iii: 1925–1930)* (London: The Hogarth Press, 1980), p. 26. One of the photographs Loeb took is reproduced by Spotts in his *Letters of Leonard Woolf*.

Woolf's hurtfulness seems all the more gratuitous when one knows that Loeb *was* a near 'professional' with his camera and that his photographic archive of the period is now regarded as unmatched. It is clearly to his credit that he was such a stickler with his tape.

Woolf's ongoing disenchantment with herself, her work, her home and her marital status in 1909 may well partially account for the acidulous tone of 'Jews', but there can be no avoiding the fact that it is an anti-Semitic outburst. After all, the heading Woolf opts for is, bluntly, 'Jews and Divorce Courts', not 'The Horrors of Dining Out as a Single Woman of a Certain Age and Divorce Courts' (or some such title), and although we should certainly read Woolf's evening out at Mrs Loeb's house in Lancaster Gate against the background of her lack of self-esteem and happiness in 1909, this only goes so far in accounting for her bitterness of tone. And even if we find mitigation for Woolf's tone we cannot skirt around her lexical or syntactic slights: that 'of course' in 'Her food, *of course*, swam in oil and was nasty' cannot be downplayed and neither can the rest of her transformation of Mrs Loeb into some kind of dishevelled grotesque. This sketch, it is important to stress, was not intended for publication (or even to be read by anyone else), but it will give offence to readers today. One can only say, with some confidence, that it was not set down with the *aim* of giving offence; the 1909 journal was not written with an eye to publication. Three years later, of course, Woolf married a Jew, but in 1909, it seems, Mrs Loeb showed acute character judgement in viewing her guest as 'severe and intellectual'.

Woolf's (relatively few) anti-Semitic smears have caused much disquiet in her admirers and much blame from her detractors, but as a number of recent commentators have remarked, many of her later pejorative comments turn into rueful acknowledgements of her own inadequacies (not exactly the behaviour of a bigot) and there was nothing exceptional about her anti-Semitism at the time. There is some evidence, for instance, that both her sister and her mother harboured stereotypical prejudices against Jews,[37] as did friends such as Rupert Brooke, Noel Olivier, Jacques Raverat[38] and Clive Bell[39] – indeed, there are many indications that such attitudes were endemic among the English upper middle class in Woolf's time. Later on, in the 1930s, Woolf would become 'very critical and analytical of her anti-Semitism'[40] and go out of her way, in *The Years*, to contest the anti-Semitism of the British Union of Fascists and to emphasise the embeddedness of the Jews in England.[41] Woolf was no dyed-in-the-wool anti-Semite, but, as 'Jews' makes absolutely clear, an element of anti-Semitism was unfortunately part of her make-up, especially in her early years. It was not, thank goodness, a dominant part

* * *

DIVORCE COURTS

'Divorce Courts' is Woolf's response to a cause célèbre. In late October 1909, Alice Mary Fearnley-Whittingstall, née Wethered, (1866–1945) petitioned for a judicial separation from her husband, the Revd Herbert Oakes Fearnley-Whittingstall (1859–1949) on the grounds of his cruelty. The

37. Lee, pp. 119 and 84 respectively.
38. Lee, p. 293.
39. Lee, p. 313.
40. Lee, p. 315.
41. David Bradshaw, 'Hyams Place: *The Years*, the Jews and the British Union of Fascists', in Maroula Joannou, ed., *Women Writers of the 1930s: Gender, Politics and History* (Edinburgh: Edinburgh University Press, 1999), pp. 179–91.

respondent, an Old Etonian who had taken holy orders during his time at New College, Oxford, and had since 1902 been the Rector of Chalfont St Giles in Buckinghamshire, denied the allegation.[42]

Opening the proceedings, Mrs Fearnley-Whittingstall's counsel advised the court that the allegations of cruelty covered a considerable period, and more especially the year 1908, when, it was asserted, the respondent had told the petitioner to leave the house on no fewer than four occasions. 'The story did not depend on specific acts, but on general conduct and on violent threats which led to a very natural apprehension by the petitioner of personal violence on her husband's part,' *The Times* reported.

The couple had been married since 25th August 1891 and went on to have six children, but difficulties had arisen in 1894 when their second child was born. 'The respondent had been warned by medical men in attendance on his wife... as to the danger to his wife if he persisted in his present course of conduct. He had nevertheless adopted a system of constant insistence on marital rights, and the petitioner had suffered in consequence. The respondent seemed to be a man who was not able to control his passionate anger any more than he could control his passions in other directions.' In March 1908, the petitioner declined to occupy the same bedroom with her husband, and there were scenes of increased violence, it was alleged, after that. The respondent also became very hostile to a Miss Gwendoline Lewis, a friend of the petitioner. Eventually, on 18th November 1908, Mrs Fearnley-Whittingstall left the marital home, as the respondent had repeatedly asked her to do, and went to live with Miss Lewis in London.

42. My account of the case is based on reports in *The Times* and on private family papers.

It further emerged that the Revd Fearnley-Whittingstall refused to speak to his wife when he was annoyed with her. He had abused her for smoking a cigarette, 'which she did by the doctor's advice', and had on one occasion threatened her with a razor. Moreover, he had continued to have children with her even though doctors had told him that this was ill-advised. He had also 'threatened to strike his wife with a crucifix and also a flower vase. He had sent her nauseating love letters, which he knew she disliked. When marital intercourse had been resumed after 1894 it had been against her will. She had lived in fear of her husband since 1902,' her counsel stated.[43]

The case continued the following day, when the court heard that the respondent's family were against the petitioner and on her husband's side because she had taken up with Miss Lewis, a professional violin teacher, who had first come to the Fearnley-Whittingstalls' house in 1908 to teach one of the boys the violin.[44]

On 28th October the court heard that the couple had had a particularly heated quarrel during a game of croquet at the Rectory and that the Rector had assaulted his wife with a mallet (it was this incident which intensified press interest in the case). 'We are dealing with very serious issues,' Mr Justice Bargrave Deane quipped at this point to the amusement of the court. '…Personally I know no game so liable to put one out of temper as croquet.' Details also emerged of a similar case in 1903 when another woman had left her husband to live with Miss Lewis.[45]

43. 'Probate, Divorce, and Admiralty Division. Before Mr Justice Bargrave Deane. Fearnley-Whittingstall v. Fearnley-Whittingstall. Wife's Plea for Judicial Separation.' *The Times* (27th October 1909), p. 3.
44. *The Times* (28th October 1909), pp. 3–4.
45. *The Times* (29th October 1909), p. 3.

The following day the respondent delivered his testimony, and this was reported in *The Times* on 30th October. Woolf visited the court on Wednesday 3rd November 1909 to hear the Revd Fearnley-Whittingstall continue giving evidence. It was the final day of the case and Woolf wrote up her impressions of it later that day. The report in *The Times* of 4th November 1909 (p. 3) confirms that Woolf would have heard him describe the relationship between Miss Lewis and Mrs Fearnley-Whittingstall as 'a perfectly unnatural friendship', and he does indeed, as Woolf reports, use the word 'solemnize' to describe his holding of a crucifix during an altercation with his wife.

Summing up, the judge (who had previously had a private word with the Revd Fearnley-Whittingstall during which he advised him to settle out of court; although he could give a verdict for him, if he did it could result in a permanent break-up of the marriage) made plain his distaste for Miss Lewis and counselled Mrs Fearnley-Whittingstall to abandon her. He refused to grant a judicial separation, commenting that he thought 'it better for both parties that there should be no judgement in this case'.

In the event, the Fearnley-Whittingstalls separated for four years before being reconciled in 1913. From then on, they lived as man and wife until the death of Alice in 1945. 'My grandparents, when I knew them as a child, seemed to be deeply devoted to each other,' Robert Fearnley-Whittingstall recalls. 'I remember my grandfather saying in 1948 or there-abouts: "I have just come back from putting flowers on the grave of my darling."'[46]

Before the court case Herbert Fearnley-Whittingstall had aspirations to be a bishop but the scandal put paid to them.

46. Robert Fearnley-Whittingstall to David Bradshaw, 3rd February 2003.

He was never offered any promotion and this was why he remained Rector of Chalfont St Giles until as late as 1942.

At one point in her 1st April 1909 review of the Carlyle love letters Woolf observes that as more is revealed of the Carlyles' marriage, 'it taxes our powers to the utmost to understand; the more we see the less we can label, and both praise and blame become strangely irrelevant.'[47] We see something of this in 'Divorce Courts'. Woolf was drawn to the court by the sensational coverage which the case was then receiving in the newspapers, but her own report on it is more understanding, more balanced than we might have expected. Unlike the earlier sketches in the journal, she is reluctant to blame either party categorically, and, if they lie anywhere, her sympathies seem to lie with the Old Etonian, the solidly Victorian cleric. Certainly she declares his wife 'the more unjust', and is particularly hard on the one figure the later Woolf might have been expected to align herself with: the lesbian Miss Lewis. In 1909, however, the grasp of class still held Woolf very tightly indeed.

47. *Essays*, i, p. 257.

BIOGRAPHICAL NOTE

Adeline Virginia Stephen was born in London on 25th January 1882, the third of four children of Leslie Stephen, a distinguished man of letters, and Julia Jackson Duckworth, a widow. Both her parents had children from previous marriages, and she grew up in a large active family, which spent long summer holidays near St Ives. Educated at home, she had unlimited access to her father's library; she always intended to be a writer.

In 1895, her mother died unexpectedly, and soon after this Virginia suffered her first nervous breakdown; she was to be beset by periods of mental illness throughout her life. Following the death of their father in 1904 the four orphaned Stephens moved to Bloomsbury where their home became the centre of what came to be known as the Bloomsbury Group. This circle included Clive Bell (whom Virginia's sister Vanessa married in 1907), Lytton Strachey, John Maynard Keynes, and Leonard Woolf, whom Virginia was to marry in 1912 after his return from seven years' public service in Ceylon.

Virginia completed her first novel, *The Voyage Out*, in 1913, but her subsequent severe breakdown delayed its publication until 1915, by which time the Woolfs had settled at Hogarth House at Richmond. As a therapeutic hobby for Virginia, they brought a small hand press, on which they set and printed several short works by themselves and their friends. The first publication of The Hogarth Press appeared in 1917, and thereafter it gradually developed into a considerable enterprise, at first publishing works by then relatively unknown writers such as T.S. Eliot, Katherine Mansfield and E.M. Forster, as well as the Woolfs themselves.

While living at Richmond Virginia wrote her second, rather

orthodox, novel, *Night and Day* (1919), but was concurrently composing more experimental pieces such as *Kew Gardens* (1919) and *Monday or Tuesday* (1921). In 1920 the Woolfs bought Monk's House in Rodmell and there Virginia began her third novel *Jacob's Room* (1922). This was followed by *Mrs Dalloway* (1925), *To the Lighthouse* (1927) and *The Waves* (1931), and these three novels established her as one of the leading writers of the Modernist movement. *Orlando*, a highly imaginative 'biography' inspired by her involvement with Vita Sackville-West, was published in 1928. *The Years* appeared in 1937, and she had more or less completed her final novel, *Between the Acts*, when, unable to face another attack of mental illness, she drowned herself in the River Ouse on 28th March 1941.

David Bradshaw is Hawthornden Fellow in English Literature at Worcester College, Oxford, and a specialist in late nineteenth- and early twentieth-century literature. He has edited a number of key Modernist texts, including Woolf's *Mrs Dalloway* and *The Mark on the Wall and Other Short Fiction* (both in the Oxford World's Classics series).

HESPERUS PRESS – 100 PAGES

Hesperus Press, as suggested by the Latin motto, is committed to bringing near what is far – far both in space and time. Works written by the greatest authors, and unjustly neglected or simply little known in the English-speaking world, are made accessible through new translations and a completely fresh editorial approach. Through these short classic works, each around 100 pages in length, the reader will be introduced to the greatest writers from all times and all cultures.

For more information on Hesperus Press, please visit our website: **www.hesperuspress.com**

ET REMOTISSIMA PROPE

SELECTED TITLES FROM HESPERUS PRESS

Author	Title	Foreword writer
Pietro Aretino	*The School of Whoredom*	Paul Bailey
Jane Austen	*Love and Friendship*	Fay Weldon
Honoré de Balzac	*Colonel Chabert*	A.N. Wilson
Charles Baudelaire	*On Wine and Hashish*	Margaret Drabble
Giovanni Boccaccio	*Life of Dante*	A.N. Wilson
Charlotte Brontë	*The Green Dwarf*	Libby Purves
Mikhail Bulgakov	*The Fatal Eggs*	Doris Lessing
Giacomo Casanova	*The Duel*	Tim Parks
Miguel de Cervantes	*The Dialogue of the Dogs*	
Anton Chekhov	*The Story of a Nobody*	Louis de Bernières
Wilkie Collins	*Who Killed Zebedee?*	Martin Jarvis
Arthur Conan Doyle	*The Tragedy of the Korosko*	Tony Robinson
William Congreve	*Incognita*	Peter Ackroyd
Joseph Conrad	*Heart of Darkness*	A.N. Wilson
Gabriele D'Annunzio	*The Book of the Virgins*	Tim Parks
Dante Alighieri	*New Life*	Louis de Bernières
Daniel Defoe	*The King of Pirates*	Peter Ackroyd
Marquis de Sade	*Incest*	Janet Street-Porter
Charles Dickens	*The Haunted House*	Peter Ackroyd
Fyodor Dostoevsky	*Poor People*	Charlotte Hobson
Joseph von Eichendorff	*Life of a Good-for-nothing*	
George Eliot	*Amos Barton*	Matthew Sweet
F. Scott Fitzgerald	*The Rich Boy*	John Updike
Gustave Flaubert	*Memoirs of a Madman*	Germaine Greer
E.M. Forster	*Arctic Summer*	Anita Desai
Ugo Foscolo	*Last Letters of Jacopo Ortis*	Valerio Massimo Manfredi
Elizabeth Gaskell	*Lois the Witch*	Jenny Uglow

Collect the entire Hesperus Press library
www.hesperuspress.com